HAUNTED PLACES

and Other Stories

Mark Allan Gunnells

SLASHIC HORROR
PRESS

Other Selected Titles by Mark Allan Gunnells

Lucid
Twilight at the Gates
When it Rains
Tales from the Typewriter
Before He Wakes
2B
324 Abercorn
The Daylight Will Not Save You

The characters and events in this book are fictitious. Any similarity to real persons, living or dead, is coincidental and not intended by the author.

PRESS

Originally published in Australia by Slashic Horror Press in 2023.

ISBN-13: 978-0-6457638-5-0
Cover design by Grim Poppy Designs
Interior design by David-Jack Fletcher
Edited by David-Jack Fletcher

This page left intentionally blank

This collection is dedicated to Clive Barker, whose short fiction taught me so much and whose queer sensibility emboldened me to explore my own.

This page left intentionally blank

Content Warning

Some of the stories contained in this collection include themes that may be triggering for some people. *Walk a mile in another man's face* contains inferences of male rape, and *Before and Aftermath* contains depictions of a high school shooting.

This page left intentionally blank

Table of Contents

This page left intentionally blank

HAUNTED PLACES

"We can't take this relationship any further."

Myles paused with a forkful of eggplant parmesan halfway to his mouth, staring across the table at his dinner companion. He and Chris had only been on a few dates, but Myles had to admit he was already quite smitten. And things had seemed to be going so well.

Chris's expression was pained, distressed, telling Myles this wasn't a joke. He sat down his fork, the bite uneaten, and smoothed the napkin over his lap. "Okay, can you tell me why?"

Taking a deep breath Chris said, "I'm haunted by my ex."

A bark of a laugh escaped Myles's mouth before he could reign it in. "I'm sorry, but...well, it's just that we all carry baggage from our past relationships. That's no reason not to take the chance on something new."

"You don't understand. I'm not speaking in metaphor. My ex died last year when he was staying over at my apartment. He's been haunting me ever since."

Myles paused a moment, searching Chris's face and finding nothing but sincerity. And fear. "You mean, like a literal ghost?"

Chris nodded, staring down at the untouched plate of pasta. "Zeke was a jealous and controlling man in life, but death has only made him more so. I like you, Myles, I really do, but Zeke won't allow this relationship to continue."

"What can an apparition do to stop us?" Myles asked. He wasn't sure he was buying this haunting nonsense, but he wasn't going to give Chris up without a fight. Especially not to a dead man.

Now it was Chris who barked a laugh, the sound grating and humorless, like a cough. A pushing up of a sleeve revealed four nasty scratches on the forearm, crusted over with hardening scabs.

Myles reached quickly across the table, taking Chris's hand. "Oh babe, what have you done to yourself?"

"Wasn't me. Zeke did this. Punishment for seeing you. If we don't stop, he will continue to punish me and he will start to punish you as well."

At that moment, as if on cue, Myles's fork flipped up

from his plate and almost jabbed into his wrist. Would have if Myles's reflexes weren't so sharp. The tines ended up stabbing into the table in the place where Myles's wrist had been only a fraction of a second before, deep enough to leave gouges in the wood.

"See," Chris said with a weary smile. "That was Zeke. He doesn't like you touching me."

Myles rubbed at his wrist, and then his wine glass tumbled over of its own volition, sending a waterfall of Merlot over the edge of the table and into Myles's lap.

"I should probably go," Chris said.

Myles started to reach across the table again but then stopped himself before making contact. "Why don't you just move? We'll find you another apartment. Hell, you can come stay with me."

Chris responded with a sad shake of the head. "Wouldn't work. Obviously Zeke follows me everywhere I go. I'm stuck with him."

"But I thought I read somewhere that ghosts were confined to the place where they died."

"That's true," Chris said, tears beginning to cascade. "And that's why I can never be free of Zeke. You see, he had the heart-attack that killed him while we were making love. He died *inside of me.*"

WALK A MILE IN ANOTHER MAN'S FACE

Gina Hatchell left the two boys sitting in the hall for fifteen minutes before calling them into her office.

Jimmy Wells came in first, walking with a cocky swagger, and Adam Gore followed, his head ducked down and his shoulders slumped. There were two chairs in front of Gina's desk, and Adam curled into the one on the left as if trying to sink into the cushions, Jimmy throwing one leg casually over the arm of the chair on the right.

Taking a seat behind the desk, Gina stared at them for a moment before speaking. "Okay gentleman, this is beginning to become a habit. I've been working as the school's guidance counselor for only three weeks, and you two have already been sent to see me four times. We need to figure out a way to end this animosity between you."

"I don't know why I'm here," Adam said in a soft, timid voice. "Jimmy's the one who's always tormenting me. Did you know that last year he knocked one of my teeth out throwing me against a row of lockers?"

Gina nodded. "I read that in your file, yes. However, I understand that the trouble today started at lunch when you called him a Neanderthal in the hallway outside the cafeteria."

"He wasn't supposed to hear that," Adam said so quietly it was almost a whisper.

Gina turned her attention to Jimmy, who stared out the window with a look of weary boredom. "Despite Adam being the instigator today, it is true that most of the incidents have been started by you. What is it about Adam that causes you to single him out for harassment, time and again?"

Jimmy continued to gaze out the window for a moment and Gina thought he wouldn't answer, but then he flicked his eyes to Adam and his nose wrinkled in disgust as if he smelled something foul. "He's a pansy. I can't stand that kind of weakness in a guy, it offends me."

"Do I sense a touch of homophobia there?" Gina asked.

Adam and Jimmy spoke at the same time. Adam said, "I'm not gay!", while Jimmy said, "I got no problem with gay people!"

Ignoring Adam for the moment, Gina said to Jimmy, "You say you have no problem with gay people, yet you call Adam a pansy?"

"Being gay and being a pansy ain't the same thing," Jimmy said. "My cousin Billy is queer as they come, but he'll also beat your ass down if you even look at him funny. Being gay don't gotta mean being weak. You can still be a man."

"And you think Adam isn't a man?"

Jimmy shot the other boy another disdainful look. "Hell no, he ain't a man. He's a walking pussy."

Now Gina addressed Adam. "What do you think about Jimmy?"

Chin still almost touching his chest, Adam glanced up with his eyes, opened his mouth then closed it again.

"This is a safe space," Gina assured. "Feel free to speak your mind."

Adam remained silent for a moment, but his entire body quaked and his face turned red, as if the words were building up inside him, expanding, causing a pressure that would soon reach critical mass. Just before he exploded, the words finally burst free. "He's a worthless piece of shit! He talks big about how he's a real man, but real men don't solve their problems with intimidation and violence. That's what little boys do, and that's all he is. A little boy playing at being a man. He may be stronger than me, but he knows I'm smarter than he could ever hope to be, and I think that's why he picks on me so much. Because he knows I'm better than him."

Jimmy lashed out quickly and smacked Adam in the side of the head. "Better than me, huh? We'll see how much better you are when I stomp your ass into the ground!"

"Enough!" Gina shouted, slamming a fist on her desktop. "Jimmy, you better watch yourself. I saw in your file that you turned eighteen last month."

"Yeah, so what? Planning on buying me a present?"

"As a minor, you've had several run-ins with the law, but you're not a minor anymore. An adult aggravated assault charge could mean big trouble for you."

"Like I give a fuck," he said, but a sudden cutting of his eyes suggested to Gina that he gave at least a little bit of a fuck.

Gina stood and stepped over to the supply closet in the corner. "What I'm hearing is that you are two young men who don't understand one another, who don't know what it's like to live the other's life."

"I don't know what it's like to be a pussy, no," Jimmy said.

Adam said nothing.

Gina pulled the props she'd made out of the closet and turned back to the young men. "Well, I think it's time you two learned a little about living each other's lives."

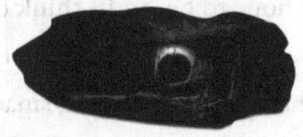

Jimmy laughed as he stared at the objects in the guidance counselor's hands. It looked as if she'd blown up the yearbook photos of both him and the pansy and printed them on cardboard, cutting them out and affixing loops of strings to make crude masks. The eyes were missing.

"What is this?" Adam asked.

"Call it a little role-playing game," Gina said, stepping toward them. "Jimmy, you'll wear Adam's face, and Adam, you'll wear Jimmy's."

Jimmy laughed again. This lady was seriously off her rocker. "What a crock of shit. Do you actually have a degree or did they hire you straight out of some loony bin?"

"It's up to you," Gina said with a shrug. "You can either go along with my role play, or the two of you can take a week's suspension. I believe one more suspension will result in expulsion for you, Jimmy."

Jimmy tried to maintain his aura of cool detachment, but he could only imagine the hell he'd get at home if he was kicked out of school. "Just give me the goddam mask!"

Gina held out Adam's face to Jimmy, and Jimmy's to Adam. "Trust me, you'll be surprised what insight this provides."

Jimmy snatched the mask from her hand and held it to his face, placing the string around the back of his head where it pressed against his skull. Through the eyeholes he saw Adam doing the same.

"Now what?" he asked, his voice muffled behind the cardboard. "Am I supposed to pretend I'm some weak-kneed sissy boy who can't even—"

Pain shot across his face, a searing heat that caused him to cry out. The stiff mask seemed to be folding in, melting and melding onto—into—his own features. He reached up to tear it away, but the mask had fused with his skin.

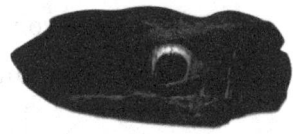

Adam felt the same pain, and when he glanced over at Jimmy, a great shock jolted him out of his chair. He was staring at his own face. Not the mask, but his *actual face*. Also, he was no longer on the left side of the desk, staring back toward the room's door, but now he was on the right, staring toward the windows. As if he and Jimmy had switched seats.

Or bodies.

"What the hell is this fancy shit?" Jimmy said in Adam's querulous voice, rising so swiftly that he sent his chair toppling over onto the carpet. He was pulling and tugging at his face—*Adam's face*—as if trying to peel off the skin.

Gina took a seat behind the desk again, her expression serene and unconcerned. "Like I said, a little role play so you can each understand one another better."

Adam walked across the office on legs that felt too long, too thin—like walking on stilts—and stood before the windows, staring at his reflection in the glass. Only it wasn't his reflection. It was Jimmy's. He raised his hand to touch his face, but in the glass Jimmy's hand rose.

"What did you do?" he said, turning back to the woman. "And how did you do it? What are you, some kind of—"

"What I am is a guidance counselor," Gina interrupted. "And that's *all* I am. At least, all anyone will believe I am. Try to convince someone of anything else and they'd just think you were crazy."

Adam saw himself getting extremely agitated, only it wasn't him. It was Jimmy, wearing Adam's body like an ill-fitting suit. "Put us back, bitch! Switch us back!"

One corner of Gina's mouth lifted in a smirk, and she said, "Nothing I can do once the masks are on. You'll have to wear them until they dissolve."

"Dissolve?" Adam and Jimmy said at the same time.

"Yes, the masks will simply disintegrate into nothing and everything will go back to the way it was."

"When?" Jimmy said, planting his hands on the desk and leaning toward the guidance counselor. He probably would have looked more intimidating if he weren't in Adam's body.

"Twenty-four hours." Gina glanced at her watch. "Everything will return to normal at 3:35 tomorrow afternoon. Until then, you get to walk a mile in another man's face. Maybe learn a little something."

Gina pulled open a desk drawer, pulled out two sheets of paper, and held one out to each of the young men.

"What's that?" Adam asked, afraid to take anything else the counselor offered them.

"Just pertinent information you'll need. Home address, parents' names, locker combination, class schedule."

"You're a fucking psycho," Jimmy said.

Gina took her purse from under the desk and slung the strap over her shoulders. "I'd say we're done here, boys. See you tomorrow."

The two young men stood side by side on the sidewalk in front of the school, merely staring at one another. Jimmy mused that staring at Adam in his body was odd, slightly off, not quite like looking in a mirror at all. But of course, that was because his reflection in the mirror was a reverse image. This was the first time he'd really got a look at his face the way the rest of the world saw it.

"What do we do now?" Adam asked, and Jimmy hated hearing his own voice sound so shaky and uncertain. "Should we go to our parents, try to explain what happened?"

Jimmy snorted a laugh. "You outta your fucking mind? Because they'll think you are. No one's going to believe this body-swapping shit. Hell, I'm having a hard time believing it and I'm actually living it!"

Adam started to cry, which infuriated Jimmy so much he wanted to punch the pansy, but he couldn't quite bring himself to assault his own face. "So we're just supposed to pretend like nothing is wrong?"

"Look geek, we only have to get through one day. After school tomorrow, we go back to our own bodies, our own lives. So I suggest we go to each other's houses, deal with our folks as little as possible, then suffer through school tomorrow until this nightmare ends."

"Yeah, but what if—"

"Jesus Christ!" Jimmy yelled. "Stop sniveling and grow a sack already. And don't touch any of my shit. When I go home tomorrow, I expect to find my room exactly how I left it."

Without awaiting a response, Jimmy stalked off, unfolding the paper and checking Adam's address. *The snooty part of town, over by the college. Figured.*

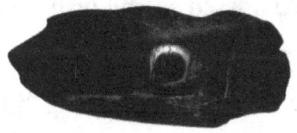

Adam checked the address for the fifth time, certain he must be at the wrong place. The mobile home before him had one busted window with cardboard taped over it, chipped cinderblocks serving as makeshift steps up to the front door, and it seemed tilted so the right end was higher than the left. The lawn was nothing but dirt, and a rusty bicycle with two flat tires and no chain leaned against the trailer. Surely no one could live here.

The front door suddenly swung open and a large, beefy woman with stringy hair filled the space. "So Jimmy, finally decided to come home?" she bellowed at Adam. "Get your ass in here right now!"

His heart slammed against his ribs like a mad bird against the bars of its cage, and he wanted to simply turn and run, but instead his feet carried him across the bare yard and up the block steps. The woman, undoubtedly Jimmy's mother, grabbed Adam by the arm and flung him inside.

He fell to his hands and knees on the threadbare, stained carpet littered with potato chip bags, crushed beer cans, and dirty dishes. Adam looked up and saw a scrawny man in nothing but boxers—*Must be Jimmy's father*—sitting on a sagging recliner staring at a football game on the television. The flat screen affixed to the wall looked to be the only expensive thing in the room.

"So why're you so late getting home from school?" Mrs. Wells said, slamming the door. "Did you have detention again?"

"N-no, ma'am," Adam stammered.

Mrs. Wells made a sound like a foghorn, and it took Adam a moment to recognize it as a laugh. "Ma'am? Did you hear that, Chuck? Suddenly our boy has manners. Think that's going to save your ass from a beating?"

"But I didn't do anything."

"Then why were you so late? Were you out with that skank you been slipping it to? What's her name, Tina? Probably got the crabs from her dirty cooze."

Adam scrambled to his knees, like a supplicant before a saint's altar. "I just had to see the guidance counselor, that's all."

Mrs. Wells grabbed Adam by the arm again, jerking him to his feet with such force that it felt like his shoulder was going to pull right out of the socket. "Why would you need to talk to the guidance counselor? You in some kind of trouble, or you been talking shit about what goes on in this house?"

Adam had never been so physically afraid in his life. Not even of his own father, and that was saying something. "N-nothing like that. I just had a problem with another kid from school."

"Fighting again, huh? You trying to get your sorry ass kicked out?"

"It wasn't anything serious, I promise."

Mrs. Wells hauled off and smacked him across the face, the sting making his right eye feel as if it might explode. She smacked him a second time and he fell back to the floor.

"I see you ain't learned nothing," she said, walking to the sofa and feeling around behind it. She brought out what looked like a wooden canoe paddle, broken off just beneath the fat end. She stalked toward Adam, who crab-walked until his back hit the wall.

"Edna, leave the boy alone," Mr. Wells said, finally getting up from the recliner. "He ain't done nothing that warrants—"

Mrs. Wells lashed out with the paddle and struck her husband in the side. He cursed and fell back into the chair. He gave Adam a helpless look, then went back to staring at the TV. He said no more.

She turned on Adam suddenly and he saw the paddle coming at him, right toward his face. He got his left arm up in time to deflect the blow, but everything from his elbow to his wrist went numb.

Mrs. Wells swung again, this time bringing the paddle down across his thighs. Pain shot through his femurs and he barely kept from wetting himself.

"You make me sick, you spineless turd," she said,

panting as if she'd sprinted a mile. "You ain't getting no supper. Get your ass to your room, and I don't want to see your
ugly face no more tonight."

Adam didn't argue, he scrambled to his feet and hurried down the hall off the living room. The first door he tried
opened onto a filthy bathroom, but the second was a dark
room with posters of metal bands on the wall. Had to be Jimmy's.

Adam closed the door and curled up on the bed. He
hurt all over and cried into the sour-smelling pillow.

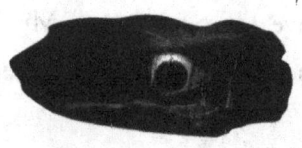

"I fucking knew it," Jimmy muttered, standing in
front of the neat Ranch style home. Red brick with white
shutters. The lawn was green and well-tended, a flower bed
right next to the porch.

Jimmy walked to the door and almost knocked. Would
the door be locked, would he have to search Adam's pockets or
backpack for a key? He tried the knob and it turned easily in
his hand. With a sigh of relief, he stepped inside.

The living room was bright with pastel-blue walls and
furniture that looked as if no one had ever sat on it. The carpet was plush, and his feet actually sank into it. Through the

archway a thin, bird-like woman rushed to him, putting her hands on him and feeling around as if for broken bones. "Oh my God, Adam sweetie, are you okay?"

"I'm fine, um, Mom."

She enveloped him in a tight hug, her stick-like arms stronger than he would have imagined. "I was so worried. When you called and said you'd had an altercation with that bully and had to stay after with the guidance counselor, I almost drove right over to the school to get you."

Of course, Jimmy thought. *Of course the pussy called his mommy to tell her why he was going to be late.*

"I'm fine," he said, extracting himself from her embrace.

"Did that punk hurt you, sweetie?"

"He gave me a good ass-whupping, but you know, that's what I get for being such a chicken shit."

"Don't say that about yourself," Mrs. Gore said, grabbing him again and placing a dozen kisses all over his face. "You're my perfect angel, and don't you ever forget it."

"Christ, stop babying the boy," said a deep, gruff voice. Jimmy looked over Mrs. Gore's shoulder and saw who he assumed was Mr. Gore. The man was tall and muscular, clutching a bottle of beer in one hand. "He needs to learn to stand on his own two feet and fight back. That's never going to happen if you keep treating him like one of your porcelain figurines."

"Shut up, Carl," Mrs. Gore said, still clutching at Jimmy. "You just don't understand the bond between a mother and her son."

"You need to cut the umbilical cord, Gloria, before he goes off to college."

"Don't listen to him," she said, turning back to Jimmy. "You must be upset. I'll run down to the store and get some ice cream and we'll talk over a couple of heaping bowls."

"I don't want any ice cream," Jimmy said, just wanting to be away from her cloying attention.

"Nonsense. I know how it makes you feel better. I'll be back in twenty minutes." She grabbed a set of keys from the table next to the door and left.

A minute later Jimmy heard a car start up outside and drive off down the street. Mr. Gore and Jimmy stood alone for a moment, just staring at one another, but Jimmy could feel the disappointment wafting off the man. He didn't blame him; must be difficult having such a pathetic waste for a son.

"I'm going to my room," Jimmy said finally and walked past the man. It took him several tries to find what could only be Adam's room. Tidy with a small desk by the window, books everywhere, and an Adele poster above the bed. God, what a girl.

A laptop sat on the desk, and Jimmy went over to it, but when he booted it up, he saw that it was password protected. *Fuck.*

He heard the door open behind him and turned to find Mr. Gore standing there.

"I don't feel like talking, Dad," Jimmy said.

Mr. Gore kicked the door closed and started unbuckling his belt. "Me either."

"What are you doing?"

"You know the drill. We don't have much time before your mother gets back. Get on the bed."

Jimmy laughed at the ridiculousness of this situation, the sound strident and panicky. "No fucking way man!"

"Do we need to go over this again? Your mother hasn't touched me in over a year, and you're a better woman than she's ever been."

Mr. Gore grabbed Jimmy by the arm. Jimmy tried to break loose, and he beat at the man's chest, but this body's muscles were so weak they may as well have been atrophied. Mr. Gore dragged him toward the bed, and as hard as Jimmy tried to resist, he couldn't.

He was tossed on the mattress like a rag doll, and Mr. Gore yanked his pants down to mid-thigh. Jimmy tried to crawl away, and push Mr. Gore off, but he hadn't the strength.

"You haven't been this rambunctious in a long time," the man said with a gravelly laugh. "I like it."

In the end, Jimmy squeezed his eyes shut and buried his face in the pillow, trying to imagine he was anywhere but here.

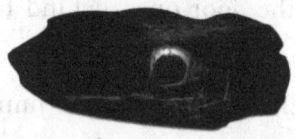

The next morning, just before the first bell, Gina saw Jimmy-in-Adam's-body at Adam's locker. A group of bigger boys surrounded him in a semi-circle, calling him names and asking if he'd almost saved up enough money for his sex-change operation. One of the boys slammed the locker while Jimmy was still pulling a book out, nearly crushing his fingers. Instead of mouthing off and scraping for a fight like he would normally have done, Jimmy pushed through them and scurried off, his head down.

Good, Gina thought. *He must be learning what it's like to be Adam, what the poor boy has to suffer daily. And hopefully Adam is learning that people who act out like Jimmy are often hiding their own secret pain.*

A satisfied smile curling her lips, Gina went into her office and closed the door.

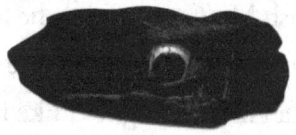

Adam stood in the lunch line, rubbing at his left arm. The feeling had mostly come back into it, but a strange tingling persisted that wasn't quite pain, but definitely wasn't normal. He'd woken up early this morning and left the house before Mrs. Gore was even out of bed. He'd expected the school day to be torture, but for the most part everyone left him alone, even the teachers.

Feeling a tug at his sleeve, he turned to find a girl with too much mascara and a tight skirt he suspected was too short to meet the school's dress code looking at him impatiently. "You got wax in your ears? I called your name like five times."

"Oh sorry, guess I didn't hear you," Adam said, but he realized he had heard her. She'd been calling *Jimmy's* name and it hadn't registered that, for all intents and purposes, he was Jimmy.

"What are you doing in line? Everybody's waiting for you outside."

Jimmy never ate lunch. He hung out with a group of auto-shop delinquents around the flagpole. He followed the girl, and was surprised when she took his hand. Was this the "skank" Mrs. Wells had mentioned Jimmy was "slipping it to"? What had she said the girl's name was? Teresa? Tanya?

"Tina," Adam blurted out loud.

She glanced at him. "What?"

"Um, how've you been?"

She stopped and turned so they faced each other in front of the doors to the quad. "You feeling okay?"

"Sure, why wouldn't I be?"

21

"You're just acting weird. First you say sorry—and you *never* say sorry for anything—and suddenly you're concerned with how I've been."

"Am I not usually? Concerned, that is."

"Did you get into your dad's prescription medication again?" she said. She lifted her hand to tuck a strand of hair behind her ear, and Adam noticed a purple bruise on her forearm. A bruise in the shape of a hand, he could even see the fingers wrapping around the underside.

"What happened?" he said, reaching out for her arm.

Tina jerked away from him, cradling the arm to her chest. "Like you don't know, you dick-weed."

Understanding dawned slowly for Adam, and with it, a rising horror. "Was it... I mean, did Jimmy do that to you?"

"So you're talking about yourself in the third person now? Who are you, Kayne West? Yes, *Jimmy* didn't want me talking to Gary Young anymore, even though we've known each other since pre-school, so *Tina* isn't talking to Gary anymore. You happy?"

Adam said nothing. What could he say in such a situation?

"Come on," Tina said, taking his hand again, probably the same hand that had left that ugly mark on her arm. Why would she put up with being treated in such a manner?

Then again, Adam thought as she led him outside, *maybe she puts up with it for the same reason I put up with what my father does to me? Because we're too afraid and weak to make it stop.*

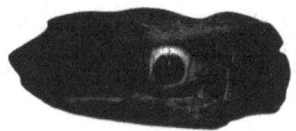

Jimmy had started out to the flagpole at lunch, but then he'd seen himself sitting with his friends. Of course, as he currently was—trapped in the body of a monumental geek—he wouldn't be accepted into that circle. It was weird seeing his group from the outside; somehow, they didn't look as cool.

He went back inside, walking slowly. He was sore, though not as sore as he would have expected. He got the feeling what happened with Mr. Gore last night was something Adam had to deal with a lot.

This morning after Mr. Gore left for work, Jimmy had tried to tell Mrs. Gore about the abuse, but she'd yelled at him to stop making up stories. He could see in her eyes that she knew the truth, but she didn't want to know. She was determined never to know. Then she'd apologized for raising her voice and smothered him in hugs and kisses before sending him out the door.

Jimmy ate lunch alone at a table in the back corner, only picking at his food as he pretended not to hear the taunts from the other kids, or feel the spit balls that pelted him in the back of the head.

After fifteen minutes of enduring the humiliation, he dumped his tray and went out into the hall, planning to spend the rest of the lunch period in the library. Adam, holding hands with Tina, had just come back inside with Pete, Greg, and Kenny.

"Look, it's Mr. Faggy McFaggerson," Kenny said with a raucous laugh. "Probably on his way to the library to look up How-to guides for cock sucking."

Everyone laughed…except Adam. At least not at first, but then he joined in.

"I need to talk to you," Jimmy said to Adam. "In private."

"You're not going fag on me, are you?" Tina said, looking at Adam. "You doing to dump me for this ass-hound?"

Jimmy ignored them, keeping his eyes on Adam. "Look, I know what you've been going through. Last night—"

Adam suddenly reached out and snatched the backpack from Jimmy's shoulder, upending it and sending all the contents scattering at his feet. "You don't know anything about me you…you…you fart-face."

All the others laughed then Adam grabbed Jimmy by the front of the shirt and pulled him close. Quietly, so only Jimmy could hear, Adam said, "Sorry, have to keep up appearances. Meet me outside Ms. Hatchell's office after school."

Then Adam flung Jimmy away so that his back

rammed into the wall. "Let's go," Adam said to the others. "Let's not waste any more time on this loser."

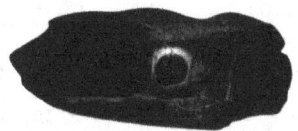

Gina checked the clock on the wall. 3:30. Only five more minutes and the masks she'd crafted for Adam and Jimmy would dissolve. The young men would go back to being themselves, but hopefully wiser and more compassionate for their time wearing each other's faces.

A commotion arose in the hall outside her office, a scuffling and the sounds of children shouting and cat-calling. She rose from her desk and hurried to the door, flinging it open to find pretty much what she'd expected. Another hallway fight, with the obligatory crowd of onlookers gathered around, jeering and cheering the combatants on.

Gina shoved aside two students and got a good glimpse of the fighters. She gasped, though the sound was lost in all the noise. Adam was lying on his back, face bloodied, while Jimmy straddled his chest, punching him repeatedly.

Reverse that, she thought. *The masks are still on, so it's Jimmy on his back and Adam doing the punching.*

Rushing to them, she tried to separate the two young men, but Adam turned and pushed her roughly, sending her onto her backside. He returned to slamming his fist into Jimmy's face, *into his own face*, but stopped suddenly as both young men cried out and grasped their heads. It made sense that Jimmy would be in pain, but why Adam?

Of course, Gina knew. She didn't even have to peek at her watch to know it was 3:35. The masks were dissolving, their identities were shifting. They were becoming themselves again.

Jimmy suddenly jumped to his feet, eyes clouded with confusion and darting around. He looked back down at Adam, who despite his face being cut and bruised and his nose sitting at a crooked angle, seemed to be smiling, blood staining his teeth.

"What the hell is going on out here?" Vice Principal Randolph said, rushing down the hall from the direction of the administrative offices.

Adam lifted an arm weakly and pointed at Jimmy. When he spoke, his voice was oddly nasally, pink bubbles forming and popping in his left nostril. "He just went crazy and attacked me. I think he broke my nose."

Randolph glared at Jimmy and grabbed him by the upper arm. "Mr. Wells, you've been nothing but trouble since the day you set foot in this school. You've gone too far this time."

"I didn't do it," Jimmy said, looking wide-eyed at Gina. "I didn't. He did it to himself, I swear."

The Vice Principal turned to the crowd. "Is that what happened? Mr. Gore beat himself up."

At first no one spoke, but then a short boy with thick glasses said. "Jimmy jumped on him out of nowhere. Adam was standing in front of the guidance counselor's office, minding his own business, and Jimmy tackled him and started wailing on him."

Several others in the crowd agreed, mostly people Gina knew Jimmy had picked on in the past.

"I want to press charges," Adam said, his lips pulled back in what most would probably see as a grimace of pain, but which still looked like a smile to Gina. "That son-of-a-bitch was trying to kill me."

Randolph looked at Gina. "I'm taking *Iron Fist* here to the office and will call for an ambulance *and the police*. Ms. Hatchell, you stay with Mr. Gore and make him as comfortable as possible."

The Vice Principal dragged Jimmy away, the whole time the young man looking desperately at Gina for help. But what could she do? Everyone had seen Jimmy pummeling Adam.

The crowd began to break apart and drift away now that the excitement was over. Gina crouched next to Adam and whispered, "Why did you do that?"

"I didn't do anything," he said. "I was the victim, and now Jimmy's going to get charged for aggravated assault.

Charged as an *adult*, and with all his prior run-ins with the law, I imagine he might do a little time behind bars. What do *you* think, Ms. Hatchell?"

"This isn't what I intended," she muttered, more to herself than to him. "This isn't how things were supposed to work out."

Adam placed his hand on hers and she cringed away from his touch. "I think it all worked out perfectly. In fact, I'd love it if you could make some masks for me and my father."

As Gina looked on, a feeling of guilt and horror growing inside her like a tumor, Adam began to laugh.

O LITTLE TOWN...

Kevin and Mike cuddled on the sofa while *How the Grinch Stole Christmas* played on the television mounted over the fireplace. Other than the flickering of the TV, the only other illumination in the room came from the twinkling red and green lights on the Christmas tree displayed in the bay window. Outside, the wind howled as snow continued to accumulate. A rare Southern white Christmas, and a blizzard to boot. Mike had checked the news online earlier, which warned the roads were icy and treacherous and people were urged to stay off the streets.

"I'm glad we decided not to go to my folks this year," Kevin said, pulling the blanket tighter around them. The gas jets in the fireplace kept the inside of the small house they owned fairly toasty, but on a snowy Christmas night, snuggling under a blanket just seemed appropriate. "Can you imagine if we'd gotten snowed in with my family?"

Mike groaned. "The only thing more nightmarish would be getting snowed in with *my* family. Not that they'd ever invite us anyway."

Kevin buried his nose in Mike's hair and inhaled his distinctive scent. "Doesn't matter. We're family."

"Only family I need. This should be our new tradition. Just the two of us, and the Grinch of course. Our own little bubble, the outside world not allowed in."

They kissed, the holiday cartoon forgotten. Mike pulled back with a smile. "Can I open my last gift now?"

Kevin frowned, glancing over at the tree and the bare skirt laid out beneath it. "We already exchanged all our presents."

"I think I've got one package left to open," Mike said, smiling widening as his hand snaked under the elastic waistband of Kevin's sweatpants and cupped the warm bulge there.

Kevin's frown tilted upward into a smile of his own. "Just call me Santa."

The two kissed again, this time with more fervor and purpose. Kevin began to slide his pants off when a pounding at the front door startled them both.

"Holy fucking hell!" Kevin snapped, quickly tucking himself back in. "Who could possibly be knocking on our door on Christmas night?"

"Really late trick-or-treaters?"

Ignoring his husband's joke, Kevin stood and started for the door when the pounding resumed, this time accompanied by someone screaming outside. "Please, let me in! Oh God, let me in!"

"That sounds like Peggy from across the street," Mike said, getting to his feet and wrapping his arms around himself as if suddenly chilly. "She sounds desperate."

Kevin hurried the rest of the way across the room and opened the door. Peggy pushed roughly past him, screaming, "Close the door! Close the door!" before throwing her arms around Mike like she wanted to tackle him, pressing her face into his chest and sobbing.

After sparing a quick glance out at the raging storm that made it impossible to even see Peggy's house across the street, Kevin closed and locked the door. He felt dazed. Peggy had bounded past him in a blur, but he had definitely seen blood on her arms and face. And that wasn't the only bizarre thing he'd noticed.

"Have a seat," Mike said in a soothing voice, helping Peggy onto the couch. Definitely blood, now smeared on Mike's white T-shirt.

Despite the blizzard outside, Peggy was barefoot, wearing only a pair of loose-fitting pants and a pink shirt that was too small for the huge protruding belly. The woman rocked back and forth, hands splayed on her beach ball of a stomach.

Mike squatted in front of her, still speaking soothingly. "Peggy, can you tell us what happened? Where's Joe?"

She looked up, her eyes frightening dull. "Joe? He's dead."

"What?" Kevin said, stepping forward.

"That thing killed him before I could even move. Ripped him apart like he was made of paper."

Kevin was about to tell Mike to call the police, but Mike was one step ahead, already grabbing his cellphone off the coffee table. He dialed, put the phone to his hear, then pulled it away to stare down at the screen. Looking over at Kevin, he said, "My phone's not getting any reception. Must be the storm."

"My cell is in the bedroom. Go try it."

Mike hurried down the hall. Kevin sat next to Peggy, reaching out to take one of the woman's hands. He couldn't really claim to be close to either Peggy or her husband, but the couple had always been pleasant enough to them. Considering Kevin and Mike had harbored reservations about living in the small southern town of Greer, South Carolina—instead of one of the bigger, more progressive cities like Asheville in North Carolina or Atlanta down in Georgia—"pleasant" neighbors had seemed a blessing that bordered on the miraculous.

"Are you sure Joe is dead?"

"He's in pieces." Peggy's voice was flat in an offhanded way, making the statement seem almost flippant. "That *thing* broke through the window and snatched him right up, then shredded him while I watched."

"What thing? Was it some kind of animal, a wild dog maybe?"

"It was…a *thing*," she said, before pulling her hand free of his, and once more cradling her stomach.

"I didn't realize you were pregnant," Kevin said, staring down at the skin stretched tightly across that perfectly round stomach.

Peggy laughed, but it was hoarse, like a dry cough. "I wasn't. Not until about an hour ago."

Before Kevin could even begin to formulate a response, Mike came back into the room and motioned Kevin over. The two met up at the head of the hallway, and Mike spoke quietly.

"Your cell isn't getting reception either. I tried the computer, but the internet is down. Cable's out too."

Behind them, Boris Karloff sang "You're a Mean One, Mr. Grinch" at low volume, the show continuing to play from an old DVD. Peggy was humming along with the tune, caressing her belly.

"I'm not sure what really happened to Joe," Kevin said. "I tried getting more information out of her, but nothing she said made sense."

"I'll tell you what else doesn't make sense. I saw her at the grocery store two days ago, while everybody was cleaning out the bread and milk in advance of the snowstorm."

"So?"

"So," Mike said, "her stomach was flat as a board then, and now she looks about eleven months pregnant."

Kevin had seen her only yesterday, the two waving at one another from their respective carports. And she had most definitely not been pregnant. "That's impossible," he said, despite evidence to the contrary.

And he was right. Peggy's pregnancy was real, he knew that, but that didn't make it any less impossible.

Suddenly Peggy stopped humming, and began screaming. Kevin and Mike both ran to find her bent forward, screeching through clenched teeth. Kevin stepped in something damp and looked down to see a stain on both the sofa cushions and the throw rug between Peggy's feet.

"Oh god, I think my water broke," she said.

"We've got to get her to the hospital," Kevin said.

Mike shook his head, more in touch with the reality of the moment. "The roads are covered in ice. We'd never make it. We'd end up in a ditch before we got to the end of the street."

"Well, we can't deliver the baby. Neither of us has any medical training apart from what we've seen on *Grey's Anatomy*. And I'm not sure that's even realistic."

Peggy screamed again, sliding off the sofa onto her hands and knees, her head bending to touch the floor like she was doing puppy pose in a yoga class.

Mike reached down for her, but then something heavy slammed into the side of the house, causing the entire place to shake. Glasses and dishes rattled in the kitchen cabinets, several ornaments fell from the tree like suicidal jumpers, and the ornate vase Kevin's aunt had given them as a housewarming gift slid off the end table to shatter on the hardwood floor.

"What the fuck was that?" Mike said, straightening up and grabbing hold of Kevin's arm.

"I don't know, maybe a tree limb fell and hit the house."

Peggy pushed up to table pose, her arms quaking as if the effort to hold herself up was nearly impossible. "I think it's the baby's father, probably wants to make sure his little one comes into the world okay."

"I thought you said Joe was dead," Kevin said through numb lips.

She turned her head and fixed him with a stare that chilled him. "Joe's not the father. That thing is."

A keening wail—separate from the wind—rose in the air, a long, sustained note that was deep and mournful.

Mike knelt next to Peggy, putting his hands on her shoulders. "What are you talking about? What's out there?"

She screamed again as another contraction tore through her, sweat dripping down her face as if she'd been doused with water. When the pain seemed to subside, she spoke between gasping breaths. "Didn't get a good look. Not all of it. Arms. So many...arms. Tentacles. Red eyes. After it killed Joe, it *took* me. So much pain, I passed out. Came to an hour later. Stomach already swollen. Phone not working. Came here for help. Now I know. There is no help."

Kevin started to say, "That's impossible" again, but stopped himself. She had clearly been through a great trauma, and perhaps she had invented some cosmic horror to better cope with it. More than likely an intruder had broken in, killed Joe, then raped Peggy. Her mind had cracked and created this narrative because the banality of the evil she'd experienced was too much to bear.

His Psych 101 explanation didn't account for her sudden pregnancy though, or whatever had slammed into the house, or that keening wail that continued outside.

Peggy let out a keening wail of her own and flipped over onto her back, clawing her pants and underwear down to her knees. Kevin tried not to look, but he couldn't help but stare at the ravaged ruin of her sex. He saw the bruising, the tearing, the raw gaping result of a violent encounter.

"I want it out of me!" she screamed, beating at her own stomach. "Whatever that thing put inside of me, I just want it out!"

"What should we do?" Mike said. "Boil some water?"

Kevin frowned. "Why, you going to make tea?"

"I don't know, that's what they always do on TV if

someone's having a baby outside the hospital. They boil water and get clean towels."

"Well, this is real life, not a TV show," Kevin said.

Mike looked skeptical. "You sure? This feels an awful lot like something you'd see on *Stranger Things*."

Something slammed into the side of the house again, and several knickknacks fell off the shelves. Kevin ran for the bay window, scooting behind the Christmas tree. He stared out the glass, at first seeing nothing but the white-out. Then a large amorphous black shape blocked the streetlights.

He got a glimpse of two burning red dots that might have been eyes, and a swarm of tentacle-arms moving through the air around the thing's body. These appendages were thick, the size of telephone poles, but bendable. He thought he saw little suction cups attached to them though it was hard to tell in the dark. As he watched, one of those tentacles lashed toward him and struck the window, creating a lightning crack in front of his face. He cried out and scurried back, bumping into the tree and nearly knocking it over. No doubt the tentacle could smash right through the window if the creature wanted. Was it merely playing with them? Did it have that much intelligence?

"What's out there?" Mike asked, his voice high-pitched and shrill.

Before Kevin could answer, Peggy screamed again, raw and guttural. Kevin glanced over to see her flesh tearing even more, and a viscous fluid, tinged with blood, poured onto the throw rug. Helpless, Kevin dropped to his knees and pulled her pants and underwear the rest of the way off. Like it or not, the baby was coming and there was no one to do anything about it but him.

"I guess you can go get some clean towels," he said to Mike.

Mike hurried toward the laundry room at the back of the house. Kevin remained in position, holding his hands out like he thought he was going to catch a ground ball. He had no fucking idea what he was doing, but he told himself that women had given birth for centuries before modern medicine, so surely the process would mostly take care of itself.

Peggy let out a strangled scream, weaker than the others. Her hair was soaked by sweat, clinging to the sides of her face like…well, like tentacles.

Kevin had a frightening image of slimy black tentacles snaking out of her vagina and grabbing him, the monster baby pulling him *in* instead of him pulling it *out*. He shook his head and yelled, "Mike, hurry up with those towels!"

Another wail from outside, and this time something slapped the roof. Kevin glanced back toward the window, half expecting something to crash through it like the possessed tree in *Poltergeist*. When he turned his attention back to Peggy, he gasped softly. Something was coming out of her. Not the tentacles he'd imagined, but a little pink dome peppered with dark hairs. The baby's head starting to emerge. What had he heard this called? Crowning, the baby was crowning!

"The baby's coming," Kevin said, but when Peggy didn't respond, he looked up to find her face to the side, eyelids at half-mast. She must have passed out from the pain. Kevin felt panic fluttering in his chest, like a bird banging against the walls of its cage. Didn't she need to be conscious in order to push? Wasn't that the directive all mothers received repeatedly in the delivery room? *Push, push, puuuuuuuuuuuuush!* He wondered if he should try to rouse her, and where the hell was Mike with those fucking towels?

Kevin gasped again as the baby's head popped completely out, and then a tiny little arm followed, hand clawing at the rug. When the other arm emerged, he realized the baby was clawing its way out. Another impossible thing he was witnessing.

Opening his mouth to call for Mike again, he heard the sound of glass shattering, and Mike screaming from the back of the house. Acting purely on instinct—for the moment forgetting all about Peggy and her demon spawn—Kevin jumped to his feet and started running toward the back of the house. In the hallway, he nearly collided with Mike, who was coming from the opposite direction, clutching a large beach towel to his chest. They'd bought it during a trip to Pawley's Island a couple of years ago.

"What happened?" Kevin asked, grabbing his husband

and hugging him tight. He buried his face in the man's hair, but instead of the distinctive Mike scent, he smelled something sour and unfamiliar. Probably the rank sweat of fear.

Mike wriggled out of the embrace. "I'm not sure. Something broke the window over the washer, but then whatever it was disappeared."

Kevin suddenly became aware of the silence from outside. Still the sound of the wind, but the wail had gone and nothing slammed into the walls or roof. Could the creature have retreated? Had it simply been waiting for its child to be born?

The baby...

"The baby!" Kevin said. "The baby, it was...I mean, it's coming."

Mike pushed past him and hurried to the living room. Kevin followed and found Mike kneeling and swaddling the baby in the towel, using the ends to wipe away the blood and mucus from its face. The thing didn't cry, but it mewled softly, and Kevin felt a chill run down his spine like a drop of ice water. He realized the mewling sounded like a quieter version of the wailing he'd heard earlier from outside. On the TV, the Whos held hands in a circle and sang "Fah Who Foraze," making Kevin realize that everything that had happened since Peggy came pounding at the door had transpired in less than half an hour. His world turned upside down in a matter of minutes.

"I think Peggy passed out."

Mike reached down and placed two fingers against her jugular. "She's dead," he said, and the lack of emotion in his voice sent another chill down Kevin's spine.

"Are you sure?"

Mike held the baby close to his chest, getting to his feet and sparing Peggy not another glance. "The baby seems healthy though."

Kevin stepped up next to him and looked at the baby. A girl. She had the old-man face most newborns did, and she sucked on her fingers as her eyes darted around, as if taking in her new environment.

"She looks *normal*," Kevin said.

Mike made cooing noises at the child. "She's perfect. A perfect little Christmas miracle, and the best gift we could have gotten."

Kevin looked down at Peggy, not quite ready to think of it as "Peggy's body". He willed her chest to rise, for her eyes to open, but she remained still and lifeless. A container with all its contents emptied out. He thought about Joe next door, ripped into pieces, if Peggy was to be believed. And now this baby, fathered by...by something Kevin's mind couldn't even conceive.

"What are we going to do?" he asked his husband.

Mike glanced up, lips spread in a smile. "We're going to take care of her, of course. We're family."

Kevin took an involuntary step back when Mike's eyes flashed red. But surely that must have been a reflection from the Christmas tree lights.

Surely.

THE BOOK HUNTER

102 Willow Lane, 1:45 a.m.

I almost killed you. Seriously, you came within seconds of death and you'll never know it, never even know I was in your house, hovering above your bed while you slept.

I had methodically gone through every single room in your house and found not a single book. Not even a stash of magazines in the bathroom, which I would have found acceptable. I ended up in your bedroom, standing at the foot of the bed. Watching you as you lay prone and snoring under the covers. I'll admit to feeling a bit of sadness, you looked like a nice enough old lady, but I had a duty to fulfill. I took no particular pleasure in it, but the rules were the rules.

No books in the house equals a death sentence.

I started around the side of your bed, pulling free the

knife, when I saw the book on your nightstand. I might not have noticed it, but the glossy surface reflected the light from the hallway. I picked it up, noting the library stamp and stickers. Of course, it made sense a person of your age on a fixed income might utilize the library for your reading. A bookmark was stuck about two-thirds of the way through.

Pleased, I placed the book back on your nightstand and left.

Interlude 1

There is no lock that can keep me out, no alarm system I cannot disable. The internet age has brought a lot of ugliness into the world, but it has also made it easier than ever to become an expert on almost any subject. It isn't the internet itself that is the problem, it is the people who utilize it. All that knowledge at their fingertips, and people choose to use it to call each other names and spread falsehoods and post pictures of naked celebrities.

Indicative of the state of the word these days. IQs seem to be plummeting, and the dumbing down of society has reached such a high (or low, depending on how you look at it) that we elected a trashy reality TV star as our Commander-in-Chief. That is what America has become—a reality TV show. I spent many sleepless nights lamenting the fate of this once great nation wondering what, if anything, I could do about it.

And then the answer came to me on one of those long nights as I sat up in bed, reading one of the hundreds of books that crowd my small apartment. I'm convinced God himself (or herself, I don't want to be sexist in my thinking, though perhaps I'm also being too binary) planted the idea. It was common knowledge that fewer and fewer people took the time to read anymore. Everyone planted themselves in front of a screen, either watching mindless garbage or surfing the web to get into anonymous fights that no one ever really won.

And so began my mission.

205 Havenbrooke Drive, 3 a.m.

I checked every room of your house twice. I wanted to be sure, but there were no books. The living room had a nice large built-in bookcase, but the shelves housed nothing but dusty knickknacks and photographs. In your bedroom closet I found some magazines, but despite the old joke, "I only buy them for the articles," I know these types of magazines are not for reading.

I find evidence that you once had a wife and two children who lived in the house, but they are not here. I like to think maybe they are readers, and that one of the reasons your marriage fell apart is because you refused to better yourself through literature.

In any case, I knew what I had to do. I made it quick, you never even woke up.

Interlude 2
I don't go out every night. That would be too risky. I also travel to many different towns in the area. So far no one seems to have picked up on the fact that these killings are connected, as the victims seem to have nothing in common. I guess people don't think to look for books in the house, or consider the lack thereof as being sufficient motive. I'm sure eventually the authorities will catch on to the fact that this is the work of one person, and maybe there will come a day when I will be caught. All the more reason to work as hard as I can now to make a difference.

1003 Frederick Street, 2:20 a.m.
I didn't even have to let myself into your house. Standing on the porch, through the window next to the front door, I could see a living room with several bookshelves full of books. With a smile, I walked back to the sidewalk and continued on.

55 Granger Road, 3:00 a.m.
I had to give this one some thought. You did have several books in your house, but they were all in pristine condition, as if they'd never been opened, lying flat with decorative plates on top of them. I could only draw the conclusion that these books were not for enjoying, but for mere decoration. Something about that struck me as offensive.

After praying for guidance, I took my knife and crept

into your room.

Interlude 3

For every house with books in it, I find five without. It can be daunting, and make me feel that nothing I do matters, that my mission won't make a dent in the stupidity that rules our nation today.

Still, they say that every journey starts with a single step, that while it make take a while, steady drops of water will eventually fill a bucket.

709 Edgemont Street, 2:55 a.m.

I did not expect to find you awake. The upside is that I found you sitting up in bed with a book open on your lap. I wanted to commend you, to thank you for being one of the precious few, but you started screaming and I had to leave in a hurry. Still, despite your fear and your misunderstanding of my mission, you give me hope.

222 Laughlin Court, 12:37 a.m.

An entire family and not a single one of you seem to read. The kids had textbooks, but that doesn't count. Those are required, though often ignored. I had to be quick and stealthy to get all the work done without anyone raising an alarm to wake the others. Messy, and again I took no joy in it. Especially the children. So much wasted potential. I tried to tell myself there was still time. They could grow up to be readers. Yet I knew that reading habits are usually formed early on. The sleeping tykes may have looked innocent, but the ignorance had already taken hold of them like a disease. So I swallowed my misplaced empathy and did my job and can take pride in that.

Interlude 4

I see my face on the news. Not exactly, but a sketch that resembles me quite a bit. I'm guessing the one I found awake on Edgemont provided the description. Didn't get everything right. My eyes aren't that close together, my cheeks not that full, but all things considered it's a pretty fair likeness.

But I can't stay in, I can't deny the task God has set for me. Even now, walking the dark deserted streets, with the police car slowing down as it passes me, I do not try to fade into the shadows. I hold my head high and walk with purpose.

I am doing God's work, the great Author of All.

Behind me, I hear the police car making a U-turn and red and blue lights wash over me. I do not run.

I merely turn and stand my ground.

BEFORE AND AFTERMATH

Interview transcript. Subject: Tyler Robert Ferguson, senior at Corinth High School. Age: 17.

It was insane, man. Just insane, like something you'd see in a movie. Not something that would really happen. But it did. No, I didn't see him come in. I was sitting in the back of the cafeteria with some of the other guys from the baseball team. The lunch period was about half over, and it was really noisy in there. I heard a few people scream, but I just thought it was some jokers fooling around, you know? Even when I heard the first gunshots, I didn't realize what they were. Then there were a lot more screams, and people started running and diving under the tables. That's when I first saw him, standing there in the doorway, holding that rifle in his hands.

He was dressed all in camouflage, like he was going

hunting, and he had some kind of black greasepaint smeared under his eyes. I didn't recognize him at first, but then I realized who it was. Ned Terp.

Ned the Twerp, that's what everyone called him. He was just standing there, shooting into the crowded cafeteria. Didn't look like he was even aiming, just firing at random, and he was *smiling*. He was actually smiling. My buddy Greg grabbed me and pulled me under the table. I looked out across the cafeteria floor, and I could see bodies. I saw at least three, lying face down, blood pooling under them.

And I saw this girl, Lila I think her name was, and she was shot but she wasn't dead. She was crying and trying to crawl away, a huge bloody hole in her back. While I was watching, another bullet took her in the back of the head. It was like a watermelon exploded, that's all I can think to compare it to. I'm not going to lie, I started screaming then myself, I couldn't help it. I mean, it was Ned the Twerp, quiet little Ned who never said boo to nobody. I didn't really know him, you know, but he always seemed like a harmless guy. Didn't talk much, was real smart, didn't have a lot of friends, but I certainly would never have thought he'd be capable of something like this. I mean, why would he do something like this? I just don't understand it. It doesn't make sense.

One month prior to the shootings

"Hey Twerp, where you goin' in such a hurry?"

Ned pretended he hadn't heard. He tucked his head down like a turtle, clasped his books to his chest, and hurried down the hall. He'd stopped by the bathroom after Algebra, and the bell had rung while he was washing up. He'd expected the halls to be deserted, but he'd spotted Tyler Ferguson and his Neanderthal buddies as soon as he stepped out of the bathroom.

And they'd spotted him.

Ned was already late for Spanish; he certainly didn't have time to deal with a bunch of brain-dead jocks out for a game of Kick-the-Ned. He'd hoped he could make it to the end of the hall before they caught up with him.

No such luck.

"Hey Twerp, I'm talking to you," Tyler said, reaching out a meaty hand and grabbing Ned by the shoulder, spinning him around. "What, don't you want to talk to us?"

Ned pressed his back against a row of lockers, trying to melt into them. There were four of them altogether, Tyler being the ringleader. They surrounded Ned in a loose semi-circle, and they all had the smirks of predators who liked to toy with their prey before going in for the kill. Ned hugged his books closer to his body.

"You know," Tyler said, "only girls carry their books that way. Are you a girl? You must be, that would actually explain a lot."

Ned looked up from beneath his tangle of too-long

bangs, took a deep breath, and said, "I'm not a girl." His voice came out weaker and more high-pitched than he would have liked.

"Oh, I beg to differ," Tyler said, eliciting cruel laughter from his posse. "Like I've already pointed out, only girls carry their books up against their chests like that. Guys carry their books down by their sides. I bet you sit with your legs crossed one over the other too, don't you? Guys cross their legs with one foot on the knee, but girls cross them one over the other. Since you're a girl, I'm betting you cross one over the other."

"I have to get to class," Ned mumbled, trying to slink off to the side.

Tyler reached out and placed a hand on Ned's chest, shoving hard. The back of Ned's head slammed into the locker and the combination lock dug into his back.

"Why you keep trying to run off?" Tyler said, and the semi-circle around Ned began to constrict. "I'm trying to help you, Twerp. It makes me very angry when you don't take the help I'm offering."

Ned flinched, instinctively tensing his muscles as if expecting a hit.

Noticing this, Tyler laughed and said, "Don't worry, Twerp, I'm not going to punch you. My mamma taught me never to hit girls."

Tyler reached out and, with a quick swipe of his hand, knocked Ned's books from his arms. They tumbled to the floor, papers falling loose and scuttling down the hall like autumn leaves. Tyler stepped on one, leaving a large footprint on the page.

"See ya 'round, Twerp," Tyler said, wagging his fingers daintily at Ned. He and his three buddies walked off, one of them kicking Ned's Spanish textbook down the hall. Nasty laughter trailed behind them.

Ned knelt down and began gathering his books and papers. Tears threatened to fall, but he held them in and allowed the red-hot anger inside to boil them away.

Interview transcript. Subject: Rebecca Leanne Martin, junior at Corinth High School. Age: 16.

I still can't believe it. I mean, I know it happened because I was there and it happened right in front of my eyes, but I *still* can't believe it. I had her blood on my arms and even my face. I just can't believe it.

Well, me and my best friend, Darla, were spending the lunch period in the library. We had this big paper due in Mrs. Weathers' English Composition class, and we needed to do some more research. It's hard for us to find time for that kind of thing, what with cheerleading practice and the Student Council and all, so we decided to skip lunch and just go to the library. I guess we'd been there about twenty minutes when we heard these *pops* from down near the cafeteria.

I thought Ricky Scarsdale was pulling another firecracker stunt. You know, like last year, with the trashcans? But then I heard all this screaming, and we could hear people running down the halls. Someone was yelling, "Call 911! He's killing everybody!" I was holding on to the belief that it was just a prank or something. I turned to Darla, and I saw nothing but fear in her eyes.

Ms. Gosnell, the librarian, was heading toward to door, I guess to check things out, when Ned Terp *busted* in. Without even pausing, he shot Ms. Gosnell right in the gut. She practically flew off her feet, sliding across the reference desk and tumbling over.

Darla and I started screaming and making our way to the back of the library. There's an emergency fire exit back there, and we were, like, going straight for it. I heard another blast and Darla, like, falls onto my back, knocking me to the floor. I rolled over and Darla's staring into my eyes, only…she wasn't. She wasn't seeing anything anymore, I could see that right away.

There was a chunk missing from the back of her head, and I could feel her blood on my skin, and it was *hot*. I almost felt like it was acid, burning into my flesh or something. I could still hear gunshots and kids screaming, so I just lay still with Darla's body on top of me. I played dead, hoping he'd leave me alone. I still can't believe it. I can't believe that Darla's dead. I've known her since I was five. Why did Ned do that? Why'd he kill her? Darla was such a sweet girl, how could he just shoot her in the back of the head like that? I just can't believe it.

Three weeks prior to the shootings.

Ned was eating lunch by himself, as usual. He sat on the pavement on the far side of the quad, his back against the brick wall of the band room. He had made a sandwich this morning, but it was soggy and unappetizing. Still, he didn't have money for the school lunch. He was chewing, staring off across the quad, when he noticed Darla Granger heading his way.

He was immediately on his guard. He didn't know Darla personally, but everyone knew *of* Darla. She was on the cheerleading squad and was dating Brock Jennings, quarterback of the school football team. She was pretty much the object of lust for every boy in school and the envy of every girl. Surely, she couldn't be coming over to talk to Ned.

And yet, she continued his way, her blonde ponytail bobbing behind her. She stopped next to Ned, smiling down at him. Her dimples were like craters in the moon. "Hi Ned," she said in a pleasant voice.

She knows my name, Ned thought, trying to form words but finding that in Darla's presence he had forgotten the English language.

"Mind if I sit down?" she asked, taking a seat next to Ned without waiting for an answer. "What are you doing over here all by yourself?"

Ned just stared at her, mesmerized by her beauty while at the same time wary of her intentions. He had learned long ago that when one of the popular kids was nice to him, it usually did not bode well for him.

"Are you mute?" Darla asked with a giggle.

"Sorry," Ned said, his voice cracking like he was thirteen years old. "Can I do something for you?"

"Do you know Becky Martin?"

"I'm not sure," Ned said, though he knew exactly who Becky Martin was.

"She's a friend of mine. That's her over there."

Ned's eyes followed Darla's pointing finger to the flagpole in the center of the quad. It was where all the coolest kids hung out at lunch during the warm weather. Becky Martin was there, tall and slender with dark eyes and black hair that fell down her back in natural waves. She was wearing a knee-length shirt that was riding up her thighs. She was a vision.

"Would you ask her to the homecoming dance?" Darla said.

"What?"

"The homecoming dance, would you ask her to go with you?"

Now Ned's suspicions were confirmed. This had to be a joke, just another attempt to humiliate Ned. "Why would she want to go to the dance with me?"

Darla sighed, her expression becoming shrewd. "I'm

going to level with you, Ned. She doesn't want to go with you. She wants to go with Tim Blanton. The only problem is her parents found out that Tim has been using a fake ID to get into bars and she isn't allowed to go out with him. However, if you asked her to the dance, she could go with you, then hook up with Tim once there."

"Why can't she just go by herself?"

"Her parents are suspicious, but if she had an actual date with someone else, that might convince them she's actually over Tim."

"So I'd pretty much be her cover."

"Exactly."

"And why would I do this? What's in it for me?"

"Look, Ned," Darla said, leaning forward to display her cleavage in what Ned was sure was a calculated move, but he appreciated it nonetheless. "I know the crowd I run with treats you pretty shitty. If you do this, you have my word that we'll back off. I'm not saying we'll all be best buds or anything, but we'll cut you some slack."

Ned thought about this for a minute. This could be a good deal for him. The assholes who tormented him daily would lay off, and he'd get to go to the homecoming dance with Becky Martin on his arm. Even if she was going to ditch him as soon as they got there.

"Okay, I'll do it," he said.

"Great," Darla said, clapping her hands. "Let's go."

"You mean right now?"

"Well, the dance is this Friday night."

Ned stood and followed Darla across the quad to the flagpole. Even though he knew this wasn't going to be a real date, that he was just being used as a means to an end, he was still nervous. His stomach was fluttering, and he felt sweat trickling down his sides. As they neared the group at the flagpole, Darla stepped aside. Ned stopped a few feet from Becky, shifted from foot to foot, then cleared his throat.

The group went silent. Not a gradual tapering of voices, just a sudden cessation, as if their volume had been turned off. They stared at him, and he felt small and pathetic under their scrutiny.

"Uhm, Becky, hi," he stammered, staring at her shoes instead of her face. "I was just wondering, uh, if you might want to go to the homecoming dance with me?"

What followed was a silence so deep it was as if the world itself was holding its breath. Ned risked a glance up at Becky. She said nothing, her face a blank mask. Then Ned noticed a twitch in her right eye, and she was suddenly spewing laughter at him. Loud and raucous and mean. Everyone around the flagpole soon joined in, their laughter deafening, an Armageddon of mockery.

"Did you guys hear that?" Becky said between guffaws. "The Twerp just asked me to the homecoming dance."

"That is rich," Tim Blanton said, placing a possessive

arm around Becky's waist. "Want to fight me for her hand?"

"Oh goodness, I can't breathe," Becky said, taking in air in big hiccuping swallows, tears leaking from her eyes. "Oh Twerp, I'd rather eat my mother's used tampons than go to the dance with you."

Ned turned to Darla, but she was laughing along with everyone else, pointing a finger at Ned and braying like a donkey. Ned turned and ran for the building, the hard-edged laughter following him inside. He was angry; at Darla and her friends, but mostly at himself. He was angry at himself for falling for their lame trick. He should have known better.

He ran into the boy's restroom near the science lab and locked himself in the far stall. He sat on the toilet lid, rocking back and forth for the rest of the lunch period, slapping himself repeatedly in the face until his jaw ached.

Interview transcript. Subject: Reginald Ernest Wallace, basketball coach at Corinth High School. Age: 37.

The doctors say they tried to save my leg, but there was just too much damage. Cut it off right below the knee. So for the rest of my life, I'm going to be a gimp, all because of that little piss-ant. He better be glad he turned the gun on himself, because if I'd had the chance to get my hands on him, he'd have been in for a world of hurt before I finally finished the bastard off.

I was in the gym, coaching the intramural basketball games during lunch. It was so loud in there that I hadn't heard any of the commotion from the school. I didn't know anything was wrong until Terp came walking in like he was some outlaw in a cowboy movie, holding that damn rifle. He must've known that I would have pounded his ass if I'd got to him, because the first thing he did was take a shot at me. Hit me in the lower left leg, and I was down for the count.

Hurt like a son-of-a-bitch, but I still tried to crawl across the gym to get to Terp. But I wasn't fast enough. He took out three kids in the gym, including Bobby Stevens, my best player. I was still several feet from Terp when he shot himself.

I tell you, that bastard just epitomizes all that's wrong with kids today. They got no respect for anything. Authority, adults, *life*—they just got no respect for any of it.

One week prior to the shootings.

Ned was sitting on a bench in the locker room, tying his shoes, when Coach Wallace walked up to him. Ned acted as if he didn't notice, spending an inordinate amount of time on a knot in his laces.

"Terp!" Coach Wallace said. "Did you shower?"

Heat suffused Ned's cheeks as he felt every eye in the room turn toward him. "No, sir," he said in a whisper.

"You think your sweat don't stink?" Coach Wallace said in a booming voice that echoed off the locker room walls.

"Is that it? You think you smell like a bed of roses after Phys Ed?"

"I don't sweat that much, sir."

"Well, I can believe that coming from you, Terp. It's not like you were doing anything out on the field today. You just stood out there in left field, picking your nose. Find anything good in there?"

The laughter from around him stung Ned like pebbles. He felt tears close to the surface, but he fought to keep his emotions in check. Crying in front of Coach Wallace would only make it worse.

"Get in the shower, Terp," Coach Wallace said, slapping Ned in the back of the head with his clipboard.

"Sir, please…" Ned said miserably, unable to articulate what he dreaded about the communal shower. He was scrawny and had acne on his back and buttocks. He could too easily imagine the boys pointing and laughing, drawing attention to all his shortcomings.

Coach Wallace squatted down next to him, his voice full of faux compassion as he said, "What's the matter, Terp? You afraid you'll get a boner looking at all the other boys' hard bodies? Afraid you won't be able to control yourself and everybody will see what a big old queer you are?"

Ned gritted his teeth, balling his hands into tight fists in his lap. Rage rolled inside him like tidal waves, but what could he do about it? If he talked back to Coach Wallace, he'd just get suspended. He could do nothing but endure it.

"Well, I'll tell you what," Coach Wallace said. "If you don't want to get naked in front of the other guys, I think I got a solution for you."

Coach Wallace suddenly grabbed Ned by the arm and pulled him off the bench. Ned landed hard on his side, his arm twisted at a painful angle as Coach Wallace began to drag him across the locker room. "Bobby, get the showers," Coach Wallace shouted.

Ned bucked on the floor like a dying fish, trying to tug his arm free of Coach Wallace's hold, but it did no good. Coach Wallace hauled him over to the communal shower stall. It was empty at the moment, but all six shower heads were turned on and spraying hot water onto the tiled floor. Steam rose like fog and wafted throughout the room. Coach Wallace yanked Ned to his feet and pushed him into the shower stall. The hot water hit him, soaking into his clothes and running down his skin, scalding him. He tried to turn back, but several of the boys were there, blocking his way.

"How's that, Terp?" Coach Wallace asked, watching Ned get drenched under the searing water with a self-satisfied smirk. "You feel good and clean yet?"

Ned curled up on the floor of the shower stall, the hot water pelting him until he no longer felt it anymore. He felt cold, inside and out.

Interview transcript. Subject: Peter Eugene Terp, father of shooter. Age: 43.

I always knew that boy would come to no good. I don't want you to think this was a reflection on me. I did the best I could raising him. His mother up and died when the boy was just six years old, and I had to bring him up all by my lonesome. I tried to instill him with the proper values and such, but it was like teaching a brick wall new tricks. There's only so much a parent can do. I don't want you thinking this was my fault.

No, I didn't notice anything unusual about him that morning. To be honest, I didn't even see him that morning. I was out late with some buddies of mine the night before, and so I slept in. In fact, didn't wake up until the police were knocking on my door. Turns out the little son-of-a-whore stole my rifle and my pickup. If I had suspected something, I swear I'd have put a stop to it. He didn't seem to be acting no different far as I could tell. Still, I always knew he'd come to a bad end, despite how hard I tried to raise him right.

Two days prior to the shootings.

The school bus pulled up in front of Ned's house. It was a dilapidated one-story clapboard hovel with peeling paint and a dirt yard. His father's rusty pickup was parked in the driveway, which meant he'd probably lost another job. As the doors opened, Ned stood and started making his way to the front of the bus. Three seats from the front, Greg Travors snatched

Ned's backpack from his shoulder.

"Hey, give it back," Ned said, his voice coming out as a whine.

"You want it, Twerp," Greg said, holding out the pack. "Take it."

Ned reached for the backpack, but then Greg snatched it back and tossed it across the aisle to Phil Westmore. As Ned turned toward him, Phil tossed the pack over to Vinnie Cedars.

"Kid, I ain't got all day," the bus driver growled, ignoring the boys playing keep-away with Ned's backpack. "I got a lot of other stops, so haul your skinny ass off my bus."

"Guys, come on," Ned said, hating the pleading sound of his own voice. "Give me my pack."

At the back of the bus, Freddie Kline unzipped Ned's pack and held it out the window, dumping the contents into the gutter below, before dropping the pack as well. Ned hurried out of the bus, the doors closing behind him as the bus rumbled on its way, the back tire running over Ned's History book. Ned gathered up his books and papers, stuffed them back in the backpack, then headed into the house.

His father was standing just inside the living room, by the window. He was staring at Ned like he would a pile of bird shit that had just plopped on his shoulder.

"Hi Dad," Ned said, just wanting to get to his room.

"I saw what went down on the bus," his father said,

nodding his head toward the window. "Those punks made a fool of you."

Well, why didn't you come and help me? Ned thought, but said nothing.

"You're fucking pitiful," his father said, his voice low and seething. "I have a hard time believing you even came from my gene pool. Sometimes I think your mother must've fucked a rooster and a turd to end up with a chickenshit like you."

"But Dad—"

"Shut up!" his father shouted, lashing out and smacking Ned in the side of the head. "Why didn't you stand up for yourself, boy? I didn't raise you to be no pussy. Why didn't you snatch your bag back and tell those boys to suck your mother-fucking cock?"

"There were too many of them."

"So what? Maybe they would have kicked your ass, but at least then you could have held you head high knowing you stood up for yourself instead of just bending over and taking it. At least then you could have proven you were a man."

"Dad, I didn't—"

"Get out of my sight," his father said, turning away and taking a swig of his beer. "I can't even look at you right now. You disgust me."

Ned retreated to his room, closing the door behind him. He curled up on his bed, thinking of everything his father had said, thinking of everything he had to endure at school. Ned's father may have been a useless drunk, but he was right about a few things. Ned *did* need to stand up for himself.

Ned needed to prove he was a man.

Interview transcript. Subject: Henry Irving Samuels, English teacher at Corinth High School. Age: 29.
I'm still in shock. When I heard the news, I just couldn't wrap my brain around it. Ned Terp is—sorry, *was*—one of my best students. He wrote the most expressive and skilled poetry. I just can't imagine him as a cold-blooded killer. No, I wasn't at school that day. I was running late that morning, and when I finally left the house, I discovered that someone had flattened all four of my tires.

I called Principal Synder to tell him what had happened, and he said he could find someone to cover my morning classes. I was supposed to come in for my afternoon classes after lunch, but by then it was all over the news.

I guess I'm lucky. I just can't reconcile what I know of Ned with what they're saying about him.

The Ned I knew was sensitive, intelligent, and had a bright future ahead of him. It pains me to know that to the rest of the world he will be remembered only as a monster.

The morning of the shootings.
Ned parked the pickup half a block from Mr. Samuels's house

and walked the rest of the way. It was before 6a.m., the sun just starting to peek its head over the horizon, but he didn't want to risk being seen by Mr. Samuels. He didn't have time to answer a lot of questions. He had a busy day ahead. A lot of work to accomplish.

Mr. Samuels's BMW was parked in the driveway. The house was dark; it didn't seem anyone was yet up. Ned scanned the surrounding neighborhood. No one was outside. Someone could be watching from a window, but he'd have to risk it. He crouched down and scuttled into the driveway, removing a pocketknife and flicking it open. He started on the side of the car away from the house, stabbing into the thick rubber tire until he heard the sound of escaping air. He did the two on that side of the car then hurried around and did the two on the other side. Wasting no time, he closed and pocketed the knife, and hurried back down the block.

He wasn't sure if his plan would work, if flattening the tires would be sufficient. Mr. Samuels was a dedicated teacher, he may just catch a ride to school when he found his car incapacitated. Still, it was the best Ned could do. If Mr. Samuels didn't stay home today…well, Ned couldn't let anyone stop him from doing what needed to be done.

Climbing into the pickup, Ned paused to place a hand on the rifle that lay across the passenger's seat. It was cold to the touch, just the way Ned felt inside. Turning away from the gun, Ned started the truck and drove off, headed for school.

MOONVILLE

Cliff followed the older man into the woods that came up to the back of the club. When they were a few feet in, the man turned suddenly, grabbed Cliff, spun him around and slammed him against a tree trunk. Cliff closed his eyes and exhaled a breath, part gasp and part moan, as he felt the older man tugging his pants and underwear down to his knees. Air hissed between his teeth as the man's callused fingers found his anus and snaked inside.

Cliff had learned about this club in the small town of Moonville on the internet, a subreddit for "hairy fun". Nothing more specific than that, but innuendo suggested he would be able to find the kind of rough trade he sought. As the man forced his hard cock inside Cliff, the full moon emerged from the scrim of clouds that had cloaked it. At the same time, the man's sharp nails dug into Cliff's shoulders and Cliff glanced behind him to see dark coarse hair sprouting all over the man's body, his clothes tearing as his muscles rippled and expanded.

The werewolf thrust deeper and howled at the moon, and Cliff howled as well.

THE TOLL

Alicia walked down the steps to the MARTA station at 9 p.m. The last train of the night would be arriving soon, and she wanted to make sure she was on it. She loved her friends, but she couldn't spend all night out at the bars with them. Not tonight, when she had a major Trig test at 8 a.m. Despite their protests and cajoling to stay and have one more drink, she'd left them to their revelry so she could get her ass back to the dorm and cram in a little more studying before bed.

The station was nearly deserted, only two other people waiting on the platform. On this side of the sunken tracks, sitting on a bench, was a young man in a cap, sweatshirt, and jeans, with a denim backpack sitting between his feet. He had AirPods. The screen lit his face in a ghostly mosaic.

Across the track on the opposite platform, one of the city's many homeless sat huddled on the concrete, back against the rough brick wall, a ratty blanket covering her to the neck despite the warmth of the night. Her face was streaked with dirt, string gray hair hanging across her face.

When Alicia first moved to Atlanta to attend Emory University, she'd been surprised and heartbroken to discover so many people living on the streets. She'd come from a small town in North Carolina, where as far as she knew, there was no homelessness. After having spent three semesters in the big city, however, she was becoming immune to the plight of Atlanta's derelict population. She didn't like to think what that might say about her.

She took a seat on a bench three over from the young man with the backpack, fumbling around in her purse to make sure she had her pepper spray handy. He looked harmless, but a girl alone in the city couldn't be too careful. She also pulled from her purse a battered copy of *The Handmaid's Tale*, which she was reading for 20th Century Lit.

She'd been reading for five minutes when to her left a voice said, "Hey, don't I know you?"

She glanced over to find the young man staring at her. He'd removed his AirPods

"Excuse me?" she said, surreptitiously reaching into her purse again, wrapping her fingers around the pepper spray.

The man smiled, revealing adorable dimples, but she

reminded herself that psychos could have dimples, same as everyone else. "You look familiar. Are you in Dr. Kramer's Tuesday/Thursday Trigonometry class?"

"I am," she said, squinting at the young man. The features under the brim of his cap did look familiar. "Do you sit in the back next to the window?"

"That's me. I'm Nick."

"Alicia. You ready for the test tomorrow?"

"Not remotely," he said with a laugh then held up his tablet. "I've been going over my notes, but it's all jumbled up in my head."

"Same here. If I was smart I'd have brought my notes with me as well. Of course, if I was really smart, I wouldn't have gone out tonight at all."

"Tell me about it. I went with my roommate to Johnnie MacCracken's for his brother's bachelor party, but I had to sneak out early."

"My friends are at the Claremont Lounge."

"Well," Nick said, flashing those dimples again, "may they enjoy themselves until the wee hours of the morning while we study our asses off."

Alicia smiled at him, feeling a faint blush creeping into her cheeks. She was always awkward in flirting situations, though she wasn't a hundred percent sure he was flirting with her at all. She'd spent half of last semester thinking she and Bobby Phillips were in the midst of a leisurely courtship only to find out he was gay.

"Since we both have to study tonight, maybe we could combine our efforts," she said, deciding to take the plunge. Even if Nick wasn't interested in her, one could never have enough friends.

The appraising look he gave her suggested he didn't play for Bobby's team. "What do you have in mind?"

"We could go to the Student Center and—"

She was interrupted by a low rumbling. She turned and stared down the tracks, expecting to see the light of the train approaching. The tunnel was dark and empty.

"Did you hear that?" she asked, turning back to Nick.

He nodded.

They weren't the only ones who'd heard the rumbling. The noise seemed to have roused the homeless woman on the far platform. She shook her head, then got unsteadily to her feet, throwing her blanket over her shoulders like a cape.

"He's awake!" she yelled in a cracked voice, revealing teeth blackened with rot.

Alicia almost imagined she could smell the stench of the woman's breath, but she knew that was only in her head. Too much space separated them.

The rumbling came again, but still no sign of the train. Alicia wondered if it could be thunder, but the night was clear, and the sound seemed to be coming not from above but below.

"He's awake!" the old woman screamed again. "Don't y'all hear him? He sounds hungrier than all get-out!"

"She's a loon," Nick said with a laugh. "That's the thing about Atlanta, you don't have to pay for your entertainment."

Alicia responded with a laugh of her own, but the sound was frayed around the edges. Was it cool to laugh at someone who slipped through the cracks and probably had undiagnosed mental health issues?

Across the tracks, the woman bent down and began rummaging through several plastic bags that had been stowed under a nearby bench. She pulled out a dented can, the kind that might contain green beans or creamed corn but had no label to identify it, and a shredded half-roll of toilet paper that Alicia assumed she probably took from a public restroom. The woman scurried over to the edge of the platform and tossed the items down onto the tracks.

"You gotta play the toll! He'll get you if don't pay the toll!"

The rumbling grew louder, and Alicia glanced back down the tunnel, sure the train must be almost on top of them. Still only darkness.

"What is that?" she asked, turning to Nick.

He shrugged. "I don't know, maybe a big truck up on the street going by."

Alicia wasn't convinced. She could now feel the cement of the platform vibrating beneath her feet.

On the opposite platform, the homeless woman began jumping up and down, waving her arms, her voice strident with panic. "He's almost here! Hurry up and pay the toll! Give him something quick, before it's too late!"

Alicia began digging through her purse again, finding an old lipstick and a nearly-empty bottle of perfume that she'd been carrying around for over a year.

"You're not seriously going to throw that stuff down on the tracks, are you?" Nick said. "The woman is clearly a nutjob."

"I know, but if this will calm her down then it's a small price to pay."

That was what Alicia said, but as she approached the edge of the platform, the superstitious part of her that kept her from walking under ladders and compelled her to toss a pinch of spilled salt over her shoulder whispered, *Better safe than sorry.*

She didn't know who the "he" was that the old woman thought was coming, but her frantic shouts suggested it wasn't Mr. Rogers.

She tossed the lipstick and perfume onto the tracks, which were about four feet lower than the platforms. She saw several other items scattered around, an odd assortment of detritus—a hairbrush, a sun visor, a Raggedy Ann doll, a compact, a notebook, condom packets, even a man's sandal. She had noticed such items littering the MARTA tracks as long as she'd been in Atlanta and never given them much thought.

Payments for the toll, she thought as she backed away.

Instead of calming down, the old woman became more agitated, pointing wildly at Nick. "Now you! There's not much time left! He's almost here!"

The rumbling was definitely getting louder, a bass vibrato that actually sounded more like a growl than thunder, and Alicia's entire body suddenly went tense as a sick sense of dread and anticipation gripped her. "You've got to have something in your backpack you can spare," she said to Nick.

"You're shitting me, right? I'm not throwing any of my stuff away just to appease some crazy old homeless lady."

"Some extra pens, a pack of gum, something," Alicia said, trying to keep her voice light, but hearing the whine of desperation coloring the words.

Nick stood, slinging his backpack over one shoulder, his tablet held down by his side in his right hand. "Look, you want to humor the old bat, go right ahead. I think I'm going to head on back to the bar and catch a ride back to campus."

"Nick, please, just do it as a fav—"

The rumbling rose into a near-deafening roar, causing Alicia to cup her hands over her ears. Nick let out a startled squeak, then seemed to slip even though he was standing still. His feet flew out from under him and he fell backward, slamming his head on the edge of the bench seat before landing on his back. Alicia started toward him, then stopped when his body began to slide along the platform toward the tracks.

"He's here, he's here!" the old woman bellowed from the other platform, hunkering down against the wall again and pulling the blanket over her head like a child hiding from the imaginary beast in the closet.

Nick continued to slide across the pavement, his eyelids fluttering. His tablet had fallen and shattered, but his backpack was still hooked around his arm, dragging along behind him. Alicia wasn't sure what was happening, at least not until her gaze traveled down his body and saw the thick black rope wrapped around his ankle. The rope pulsed and undulated like flesh, and as Alicia's eyes moved further down she realized it wasn't a rope at all. It was some sort of tentacle. It grew fatter as it neared the edge of the platform, the underside covered in tiny suckers that opened and closed as if tasting the air. The thing was the size of a small tree trunk where it disappeared below the platform.

This can't be happening. I must be losing my mind.

Nick began to groan, but his eyes didn't open all the way, stuck in a semi-unconscious state as he was dragged toward the tracks.

Forcing away the paralysis that clutched her, Alicia ran toward Nick, meaning to grab his arms and play tug-of-war with the tentacle if she had to, but she'd only gotten a few steps when another tentacle rose up from the tracks and lashed out at her. The thing hit her across the chest with enough force to drive her back and off her feet. She landed hard on her rear-end, her teeth coming down on her tongue and causing her mouth to fill with the coppery taste of blood.

Alicia watched in stunned horror as Nick reached the edge of the platform, and his lower legs dropped out of sight. At the last moment, he came to, flipping over onto his stomach and clawing at the cement. He spotted Alicia and started yelling, "Help me! Please help me!"

She felt frozen, the pain in her chest from the tentacle's impact making it hard to catch her breath. She put her hands over her ears again, now trying to block out not only the roar that rent the air, but Nick's screams as well.

The second tentacle, the one that had struck her in the chest, wrapped itself around Nick's throat, and then he was pulled down onto the tracks. His voice rose in a high-pitched shriek that sent needles of ice drilling into Alicia's brain, and then cut off abruptly. The roar also stopped, silence returning with startling suddenness.

She wasn't sure how long she sat there, her legs pulled up to her chest as she whimpered and rocked. Across the tracks on the other platform, the homeless woman emerged from her blanket cocoon and began gathering up her plastic bags. "Fool boy, I told him to pay the toll," she said. "You gotta pay the toll, you just gotta! Them's the rules!"

Without a glance back in Alicia's direction, the woman took her belongings and hurried to the stairs up to street level, leaving Alicia alone in the station.

After a few more moments, she worked up the nerve to crawl forward to the edge of the platform, glancing down at the tracks. She braced herself to see Nick's mangled body, but there was no sign of him, and no sign of whatever creature the tentacles had belonged to. In fact, the only sign of anything amiss was Nick's backpack, ripped and shredded, stained with blood.

A rumbling made Alicia scream, thinking the creature was returning for her—having found the lipstick and perfume insufficient payment—but then she glanced to her right and saw the light of the train approaching.

She scrambled to her feet and fled for the stairs.

MESSAGES

The beach was deserted as David made his way across the sand.

Not surprising, considering it was 2 a.m., and David had come seeking solitude. He'd come to feel closer to Greg, and Greg had always said there was a special magic about the beach at night—something it didn't possess in the light of the sun.

The powdery sand became wet and compacted as he neared the shoreline, his bare feet sinking a little with each step. The water rushed up over his ankles, cool and soothing, dampening the cuffs of his pants. As he stared out at the dark, rolling waves, the lights of a few distant boats twinkling like earthbound stars, David knew Greg had been right. There was magic here.

He sat down on the sand, letting the surf surge up around his legs, breathing in the salty tang of the air. To be honest, David had never much cared for the beach, preferring the mountains instead, but it had been one of Greg's favorite places in the world. So they'd compromised, spending half their vacations in the mountains and half at the beach.

When Greg had gotten sick last year, he'd wanted to see the ocean one last time, but the doctors had said traveling wasn't a good idea. Greg had pleaded, but David had sided with the doctors. A decision he'd regretted every day since Greg died. Which was why David had brought Greg's ashes to the beach and released them into this very ocean.

Exactly a year ago.

Some people have a grave to visit, I have the Atlantic Ocean. Maybe it will become an annual pilgrimage for me.

David didn't know if he'd really come here every year; he hadn't even intended to come this year. Yet as the anniversary of Greg's death approached, he found himself wanting to be close to his late husband. Since that wasn't possible, coming to the place where he'd laid his remains to rest seemed the next best thing.

Rest, David thought with a laugh. As he looked out at the constantly roiling waters, he thought there was nothing restful about the ocean. Which was somehow perfect. In life, Greg had been a boundless well of energy, always on the go, never satisfied with sitting still for too long. That was one of the worst parts of watching the sickness progress—it had stilled that which seemed incapable of being stilled.

"You'll never be still again," David said out loud, feeling like a fool, even though no one was around to hear him.

Not even Greg.

This thought brought stinging tears to his eyes. His husband's death hadn't done anything to shake David's conviction that there was no God (or Zeus or Odin or L. Ron *fucking* Hubbard), but for the first time in his adult life it had made him *want* to believe. Made him wish he was a Mulder instead of a Scully. It would have been comforting to think that somewhere out there Greg still existed.

As the next wave rolled in over his lower extremities, David splashed his hand in the water, then brought the salty brine to his lips. If Greg still existed anywhere, it was here, in the sea where his ashes had been scattered.

Of course, David knew that was ridiculous, but life without Greg was ridiculous. Now he understood the pull of religion. The beliefs might be silly, but maybe only silly fictions could combat the painful realities of the world. If meaning couldn't be found, perhaps a fabrication of meaning could suffice. Maybe you could know something wasn't real and still get some kind of value from it.

As David contemplated these philosophical concerns, staring up at a tattered, cloudy, starless sky, another waved crashed over him and he felt something bump against his crotch. He glanced down to find a dark green bottle nestled in the V of his legs, a crude cork stuck in the opening.

With a frown, he picked up the bottle. It was large—larger than the average wine bottle—with no label or any markings. The glass was opaque so that he couldn't see what, if anything, was inside. He held the bottle next to his ear and shook it. No sloshing of liquid, which meant the cork was securely jammed into the opening. He did hear a faint rattling, however, so it wasn't completely empty.

He grabbed the cork and yanked. At first the thing didn't budge, so he renewed his grip on the bottle with his left hand. Strained himself until the cork popped out so suddenly that he nearly fell back onto the sand. He upended the bottle and let the contents fall into his left palm.

Two items. A piece of yellowed paper, rolled up and tied with twine, and a stub of a pencil.

"Message in a bottle," he murmured to himself. "How Nicholas Sparks can you get?"

After plunking the bottle into the sand and twisting it several times to anchor it so the tide wouldn't carry it back out, he broke the twin and began to unfurl the scrap of paper. The absurd thought popped into his mind, *What if it's a message from Greg?*

Ludicrous, he knew, but he still felt a rush of anticipation as he looked down at the words scrawled on the paper. The handwriting was sloppy, almost as if the author's hand had been shaking, printed in all caps. David read the note's three lines several times. It seemed an odd bit of poetry, but affecting for all its oddity.

"FROM MY VANTAGE, THE WORLD ABOVE SEEMS LONELY AND FULL OF PAIN. I CAN WIPE ALL THAT AWAY. I MERELY NEED TO BE INVITED."

"Lonely and full of pain, that sums up my life," David said to the night.

Since losing Greg, he'd gone through the motions of getting on with his life, but each day was a struggle. Each day was a chore. Each day was a void. And he realized his experience wasn't particularly unique. Everyone harbored some secret anguish, some hidden suffering. This knowledge, however, didn't unite the world but seemed to drive everyone further apart, into their own separate bubbles of grief and heartache. If only there was someone who could wipe all that away.

David turned the note over, and using his palm to bear down on, he wrote, "Come on up," pressing so hard with the dull pencil tip that he tore through the paper in several places. Then he popped the note back into the bottle, replaced the cork, and tossed it into the waves. In the darkness, he lost sight of it almost as soon as it left his hand, but he heard the *splash* as the bottle hit the water.

He pushed himself up. From the waist down, he was drenched and caked with muddy sand. He stared out at the black ocean, doing its eternal dance, the sound of the waves like the universe shushing the world because there was no one to hear its collective cry for help.

As he started away from the water, imagining some angsty teenager writing that bit of cryptic poetry and putting in the bottle, the roar of the surf behind him increased. It sounded like thunder suddenly, a constant rumbling increasing in pitch.

David turned back slowly to see the water churning and thrashing, like a swimming pool during an earthquake. Not that he'd ever seen this in person, only in the movies. The waves began to crash onto the sand with greater force, moving further up the shore.

Tsunami, was the first thought to come to David's mind. Yet that was impossible, he'd never heard of a tsunami hitting the east coast of the United States.

There's a first time for everything. No one had ever heard of AIDS until the first time someone got infected.

David knew he should run, but he remained transfixed by the increasing violence of the sea. If it was in fact a tsunami, he doubted he could outrun it anyway.

As he watched, he realized that something seemed to be rising from the waters, several miles from shore. He couldn't make out specifics, but it was large, rising toward the overhead clouds, the shape a darker silhouette against the darkness of the night. He thought he could make out the shape of a torso—a head, arms—and a strange three-pronged, fork-like instrument held even higher.

Is that a trident?

For a moment, David thought other forms were rising from the ocean around this thing, but then he realized these were waves, lifting higher than any he'd ever seen, perhaps hundreds of feet. The dark shape lowered its arms, and the waves began to advance toward the shore as if in a race to see which could reach land first.

His paralysis finally released him, and David turned to sprint back toward steps that would lead him up to the parking lot where he'd left his car. Behind him, he heard the rumble of the approaching waves and realized his attempt to flee was probably futile, but still his legs pumped. In the near-by hotels, he saw lights coming on in windows as the tumult awakened vacationers who no doubt were pushing aside curtains to see what caused the noise. He imagined there would be screams and prayers.

Even in the blackness, David sensed an even deeper shadow falling over him, and a few feet from the wooden steps, he stumbled and fell face-first into the sand. As the pounding of the sea filled his ears and he felt the spray of the advancing waves, his last thought was, *I guess there is a god after all.*

THE BOY IN THE POND

Hudson didn't like the snow. He didn't like the winter months, period. In his profession as a paranormal problem-solver, he had faced down any number of ghosts, poltergeists, even a few demons, but none of them bothered him like frigid weather. Probably came from his upbringing in a dirt poor family where the house was always cold, a single kerosene heater trying in vain to warm the entire family. The cold was merely a reminder to him of the past he had escaped and wished to forget.

Shaking his head to clear away such useless, maudlin thinking, Hudson continued down the hill, his legs sinking knee-deep in the snowdrifts. He wished he'd worn thicker pants, and maybe a ski-mask, and earmuffs, and scarves wrapped around him, until he looked like a mummy. Mr. and

Mrs. Fennimore walked ahead, Mr. Fennimore carrying their ten-year-old daughter, Katie, in his arms. The girl wore only a jacket and red tights to combat the freezing temperature, yet she seemed not at all uncomfortable. Hudson mused that those who had always had money and knew nothing of want had no need to fear the cold.

The Fennimores halted abruptly, and Mrs. Fennimore pointed down the slope. "It's just there. We don't really want to get any closer."

Hudson grunted and continued past them. At the bottom of the hill was a small pond, roughly egg-shaped and not quite as large as a football field. It appeared to be completely frozen over, but Hudson didn't want to take any chances. He got down on his hands and knees and scooted onto the very edge of the pond, moving slowly and being hyper vigilant for the sound of cracking or fissures opening in the ice under him. He didn't have to go far before he found the boy.

Even though Hudson knew what to expect, the sight was still shocking. A small boy of five or six floating on his back beneath the ice, his eyes wide and empty as they stared up, as if through smudged glass. He wore a thick bubble coat and mittens. His skin was blue.

"And you say he died a year ago?" Hudson called to the family.

Mr. Fennimore answered. "Yes, almost a year exactly. The kids had come out to play. We've told them a million times not to go out on the ice of the pond, but Katie said Randall was showing off, trying to impress his big sister, and he walked out onto the pond and the ice cracked and he fell right through. She ran screaming back to the house, but by the time we made it down here...well, it was too late."

Hudson nodded and turned back to the boy beneath the ice. The boy who was not really there at all. His body had been recovered from the pond a year ago and buried in the family plot out at the Highlands Cemetery. Hudson knew all this from the research he always did after taking a case. What he saw through the ice was a revenant, a spirit who had not yet moved on. He'd never heard of a ghost haunting a pond before, but in his career, he'd learned to expect the unexpected.

"You discovered this last week?" Hudson asked.

"Yes," Mrs. Fennimore said. "You'd think after what happened, we'd not want to come anywhere near the pond, but actually it became habit for my husband and I to come down here. A ritual, I guess you could say. Somehow it made us feel closer to Randall, like a pilgrimage or something. Last Thursday we came down and the pond had only just started to ice over. I spotted him first and thought it was a hallucination, but then Kent saw it too. We both scurried back to the house, trying to figure out if what we'd seen was real or just some kind of shared delusion."

"Two days passed before I worked up the nerve to come back to the pond," Mr. Fennimore said, seamlessly taking up the narrative as if it had been practiced. "He was still there, just as before, just as he is now. I didn't know what to do, but then I remembered our friend Kevin Shaw had mentioned some work you did for him."

Kevin Shaw...Hudson had to run the name through the old computer between his ears a few times before he could pull up the facts of the case. Kevin Shaw was a well-to-do architect who had hired him a year and a half ago to evict a couple of stubborn, mischievous specters attached to a home Shaw was renovating. Hudson hadn't been able to actually eject the spirits from the house, but he'd managed to bind them so they were incapable of manifesting and effecting the physical environment.

Another satisfied customer recommending him to others. That was how his business grew. He did not advertise, he did not have a website. And fuck social media. He got work strictly through word of mouth and gaining a reputation as a man who knew his trade. That was exactly how he liked it. Helped keep his clientele exclusive and kept the riffraff away—Hudson's services did not come cheap.

With a finger, Hudson tapped lightly on the glass. The boy's spirit did not react. A residual haunting was Hudson's initial assessment, not a spirit with real consciousness or intent, merely a revenant stuck in a loop. Although, Hudson had never known a haunting of any type to be seasonal, but again, he didn't pretend he knew everything about the supernatural world. Every case taught him something new.

He started to back off the ice but then he detected movement in his peripheral vision, and his eyes darted back to the boy. At first, he thought he was mistaken, that there was no movement, but then his gaze focused on the boy's blue lips. The lips were moving, as if he were speaking under the ice. Hudson lowered his head closer but there was no sound. He squinted, trying to make out the boy's word. A single word. Hudson was no lip reader, but it seemed the boy was saying, "Savor" over and over. Or possibly, "Savior." Neither one made much sense.

With a frown, Hudson scuttled off the ice, the cold freezing him right through to the bones. Returning to the Fennimore family, he said, "I think he wants to communicate, but it may take a little time for me to find the right method to get the message. I'm sure—"

"We don't want to communicate!" Mr. Fennimore said loudly.

Hudson blinked, momentarily taken aback. Rarely was he surprised, but it was even more rare that people didn't desperately want to receive messages from loved ones who had passed on. "I'm sorry, I assumed you'd want to know what your son—"

"That's not our son!" Mrs. Fennimore said in a strident tone. "I don't know what that is, but our son is gone."

Katie had begun to cry, her face buried in the crook of

her father's neck.

"Just get rid of it," Mr. Fennimore said, his voice hoarse with emotion. "We'll pay you whatever, as long as you make that thing go away."

Hudson glanced back at the frozen pond. From this vantage point, the spirit was little more than a vague shadow beneath the ice. Finally he turned back to the family and said, "Okay, let me think on the problem tonight, and I'll be back tomorrow to take care of everything."

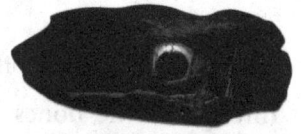

Hudson sat alone in the dark. He reclined on his sofa, feet on the coffee table, the only light filtering in from the streetlamps outside. No TV flickered, no music played. He needed quiet and dimness—in short, a total lack of sensory input—to do his best thinking. A depravation tank would have been ideal.

Behind his eyes, he kept replaying the image of the boy in the pond mouthing the word "Savor" or "Savior." What could it mean? Was he trying to tell his parents not to waste any more time mourning him, to savor their lives instead? Did he see Hudson as his savior, someone who could get him out of the purgatory in which he was stuck so that his spirit could move on?

Mr. and Mrs. Fennimore weren't interested in what Randall had to say from beyond the grave, however, and the client was always right. He held that up as his personal philosophy and professional mission statement. It ensured happy customers who would recommend him to their friends and family.

Still, his natural curiosity persisted. He found mystery irresistible, which was what got him into this line of work in the first place. However, in order to complete the job and get his paycheck, his focus should be elsewhere.

With a sigh, he stood and left the living room, going down the hall to the bathroom. The cliché went that most wouldn't want to be in a single man's bathroom, but Hudson was the exception to that rule. Fastidious by nature, his entire house was tidy and neat, but no room more so than his bathroom. The linoleum tiles shone, the porcelain of the sink, tub, and toilet gleaming. No splashes around the bowl, no mildew on the shower-stall glass. The bathroom had the sterile look and feel of an operating room. Bypassing the shower stall in the corner that looked a little like an old-time phone booth, he went to the large, round garden tub. Sitting on the rim, he placed the stopper in the drain and turned on the water. Nothing relaxed him like a long soak in the tub.

As he waited for the tub to fill, steam rising in the air like ethereal phantoms, he slowly undressed, folding his clothes and placing them neatly on the closed toilet seat. He stared into the mirror above the sink. He wasn't actually study-ing his reflection, rather he was mulling over the problem of how to get rid of little Randall's spirit.

There were a multitude of reasons why a spirit may not move on. A sense of unfinished business was the most common, but sometimes the person was merely confused and lost, unable to accept or comprehend that they had died. With a child so young, that seemed the most likely. Mortality was a concept a five year old had trouble grasping, so the spirits of children often lingered long after their deaths.

And they were the hardest to get rid of, because they lacked the reasoning skills of adults. Hudson would have to adjust his normal approach, try to put himself in the mind of a five year old, the types of arguments they would find com-pelling. In the past, he'd had success ushering children's spirits off this plane by promising that pets and favorite stuffed ani-mals were waiting for them. Manipulative yes, but it got the job done.

Turning back to the tub, he twisted the faucet handles and prepared to step into the warm water, but then glanced down and let out a shocked gasp, backing away. Hudson felt something he rarely felt—fear. Risking a peek back in the tub, he confirmed what he'd seen before.

Randall, floating beneath the water.

While this was not entirely unprecedented, it was ex-tremely rare. Despite what the movies and those "true life" documentary shows suggested, ghosts did not routinely follow people home. Fact was, spirits were usually tied to a specific place, and in a few cases, a specific person. They did not typically do much traveling.

Once the shock wore off, Hudson snapped back into investigator mode. Settling on the edge of the tub, he placed a hand in the water and splashed it around. The boy's image wavered and quivered, but as the water stilled, the boy regained focus and seeming solidity. He began moving his mouth again, the same word repeated soundlessly. Since the spirit had left the pond and followed Hudson home, he was inclined to believe the word was "Savior" and that the boy was crying out to Hudson for help.

And Hudson planned to do his best.

He leaned forward, dipping his head so close to the surface that his nose almost touched the water. "Randall," he said loudly and clearly. "I want you to listen to me. You've died. You fell through the ice in the pond and you drowned. You're not alive anymore."

Real elementary stuff, but he was dealing with a child. Randall had died when he was barely more than a toddler. Hudson would have to keep it as simple as possible in order to get through to the spirit.

The boy did not react to Hudson's words, just continued to stare up through the water and mouth the word over and over.

"Randall, your parents love you and they miss you, but you can no longer be with them. You have to move on. There's nothing for you here anymore. Something waits for you on the other side, and you need to go through that door. There will be toys and candy and rides, and your family will meet you there later."

Pretty lies, but sometimes a lie was the kindest bit of mercy.

"Can you hear me, Randall?" Hudson asked, leaning forward just a little bit more. "You need to—"

The boy's hands shot out of the water and grasped hold of Hudson's neck. The grip was like a vise and Hudson found himself unable to breathe. He raised his own hands to try to free himself, but he lost his balanced and fell forward into the tub.

He plunged through the water, expecting to hit the bottom of the tub, but instead he just kept on plunging. The water should have been warm, but instead it was frigid with chunks of ice floating in it. Hudson thrashed about, reaching for the sides of the tub, but he found nothing. He seemed to be submerged in a vast expanse of water, nothing as contained as a bathtub. The water was dingy and cloudy, with sticks and leaves drifting past his eyes.

Hudson felt terror that froze him even more than the icy water, but a detached part of him realized it wasn't his own terror that gripped him. At least not entirely. He was feeling the terror of another. Of a small child. Terror and confusion and anger. A sense of injustice, of being mistreated and tricked and abused. Pain and rage, also a deep overwhelming concern for the wellbeing of another. A fear that this other would be harmed…as he was.

Kicking and swimming toward the surface, a wavering image standing next to the water gradually began to resolve itself until he could clearly make out Katie's features.

Hudson broke the surface and found himself in the tub, the warm water splashing over the rim to splatter the bathroom floor. He gasped and gulped air into his lungs, leaning his head against the back of the tub, waiting for his heartbeat to settle back to normal.

Randall had communicated with him, letting him know his death had been no accident. He had been murdered, and he'd returned to stop someone else from meeting the same fate.

"Not savor or savior," Hudson muttered to himself. "*Save her!*"

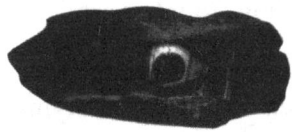

Hudson stood in the Fennimore's living room, watching the family with shrewd, calculating eyes. Katie seemed ill at ease, withdrawn and sullen. Had she really been with her brother when he died? If so, Katie had to know the truth of what had happened out at the pond. Hudson noted how the girl flinched away anytime Mrs. Fennimore went to touch her. Did she fear her mother? Could Mrs. Fennimore be the one responsible?

Then again, Katie seemed to cling to her father in a way that went beyond the usual closeness of fathers and daughters. Could their relationship be too close, *unnaturally close*, and had Randall possibly seen something he shouldn't have and therefore had to be silenced by his father?

So many questions, and no answers. Not yet.

"We don't have to go back down to the pond, do we?" Mrs. Fennimore asked, twisting a washcloth in her hands. "I just don't feel up to it today."

"I don't require your presence," Hudson assured her. "Actually, I need to be alone with the spirit. With any luck, he will have moved on before the sun goes down. As soon as I figure out the message he is trying to impart."

"I don't care about any message!" Mrs. Fennimore screamed, tears spilling from her eyes. Mr. Fennimore got up from the couch where he'd been holding Katie and ran to his wife, embracing her. Katie started crying as well and disappeared down the hall.

Hudson was not naturally a sensitive man, but he mustered as much kindness as he could. "I know you aren't interested in whatever message your son may have, but I'm afraid he won't be able to move on until he is sure that message is heard."

Mrs. Fennimore broke out of her husband's arms and said, "I'm going to take a bath." Then she disappeared down the hall as well.

Hudson and Mr. Fennimore stood staring at one another in silence for a moment before Hudson said, "I'm going to get to work."

Mr. Fennimore nodded but said nothing.

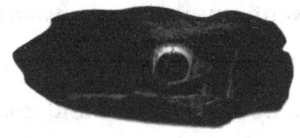

Hudson descended the slippery, snowy slope to the pond. He'd dressed warmer this time, even down to the long thermal underwear beneath his pants. The boy still floated just beneath the ice. Once again, Hudson crawled cautiously across the frozen surface until he was above Randall. The boy's mouth continued to form the words. "Save her! Save her! Save her!"

"I need your help," Hudson said, the cold seeping through his thick coat and leather gloves, reminding him of those bitter December nights as a child when he'd huddled as close to the kerosene heater as possible, but never succeeding at shaking the bone-deep cold. "I want to save her, but I need to know where the danger is coming from. Who killed you? Your father or your mother? Who is going to hurt your sister? I need you to show me. Can you do that?"

At first nothing happened, and Hudson was preparing his next plea to the spirit, but then he heard a crackling, like cellophane being crumpled in someone's hands. Too late he realized that this was the sound of the ice cracking and splitting open. He tried to scuttle back onto the ground, but he'd barely begun to move when the ice beneath him shattered like glass and he crashed into the pond.

Hudson squeezed his eyes shut and held his breath. His entire body went numb in an instant, and though his brain sent signals to his limbs to move and swim and carry him to the surface, he felt nothing and could not be sure he moved at all. In all likelihood he was sinking to the bottom like an anchor. His lungs began to burn; he resisted as long as he could then opened his mouth, bracing himself for the gush of water down his windpipe. Instead, there was only air. Air frigid as icicles, but air nonetheless.

Opening his eyes slowly, squinting against the glare of the sun on the snow, he found himself not in the pond but standing on solid ground next to it. Something about his perspective seemed off, and he looked down at his body. Only it wasn't his body. It was the body of a small child, in a bubble coat and mittens.

"I double-dog-dare you to do it," said a high-pitched

voice behind him.

Hudson turned and looked up at Katie Fennimore.

I'm seeing through Randall's eyes. He's showing me his final moments of life so I'll know what happened to him.

The voice that came out of Randall's mouth was tired and scared and a little whiny. "I don't wanna."

Katie put her hands on her hips and glared at him. "You a chicken? Is that it?"

"Mommy and Daddy said not to go out on the ice."

With an annoyed *hmpf,* Katie pushed past Randall and stepped onto the frozen surface of the pond, walking about a foot out, then turning around and returning to the boy's side. "See, it's safe as houses. Now you do it."

"I still don't wanna."

"You're such a little pansy," Katie said with an ugly sneer. "No wonder Daddy calls you his favorite *daughter.*"

"He doesn't say that!"

"Not to your face, but when you're not around he does."

Randall turned and looked at the ice again, taking a deep breath and starting forward.

Don't do it, kid! Hudson thought, though he knew he had no power to change the outcome. This was a play already written and performed; he was merely watching a recording of it.

The boy walked out onto the ice, his feet slipping and

sliding a bit. He walked only half the distance his sister had covered, then turned around. "Okay, is this good—Hey, Katie, what are you doing?"

The girl stood at the edge of the pond, a large rock in her gloved hands. Her eyes were empty and cold, her expression blank. "I got all Daddy's attention before you came along," she said in a flat tone. "And I'll have it all again once you're gone."

Before Randall could say anything, Katie tossed the rock out onto the ice. It punched a hole through, and suddenly the sheet on which the boy stood fissured with lightning cracks, and he crashed through into the cold water.

At that instant, Hudson's perspective shifted. He was now inside a bathroom he'd never seen before with black-and-white checkered tile, lemon-yellow walls, and a claw-footed tub. Mrs. Fennimore reclined in the tub, shaking and jerking as if having a seizure as the water lit up with electric blue light. A power cord snaked out of the tub, and Hudson followed it to the socket above the vanity.

Hudson cried out, his hands slipped, and he nearly banged his nose on the ice.

He was back where he started, crouching on hands and knees above the spirit of Randall. The boy continued his silent mantra: "*Save her! Save her! Save her! Save her!*"

Hudson scrambled back to solid ground and began making his way up the hill as fast as he could, tunneling through the drifts. He felt like Sisyphus, rolling that stone to the top of the mountain. A distance of a few yards now seemed like an endless stretch of miles. He fumbled in his coat pocket for his cell phone before remembering that he'd left it in the car.

After what felt like hours but was probably no more than five minutes, he finally reached the top of the hill and sprinted toward the house. He stumbled and slid on an icy patch, falling to his knees. Pain shot through his left knee and ankle, but he leaped back up and continued on.

He burst through the front door. Mr. Fennimore had been settled on the sofa, a book open on his lap, but he jumped to his feet, the book tumbling to the floor, when Hudson stormed in.

"What's going on? What's the matter?"

Hudson didn't waste time answering, just rushed through the room and down the hall. Mr. Fennimore followed close behind.

Only the door at the very end of the hallway was closed, and Hudson knew instinctively this was the bathroom. He bounded inside and saw the chess-board tile from his vision, the canary walls, and Mrs. Fennimore reclined in the tub, a sleep mask over her eyes. Katie stood just behind her, holding a hair dryer in her hands. A hair dryer plugged into the socket above the little vanity.

Even as he crossed the threshold, the girl tossed the

hair dryer into the air. Hudson dove forward, swiping out with his hand and unplugging the appliance mere seconds before it dropped into the water.

Mrs. Fennimore sat up quickly, water sloshing over the side of the tub, and removed the mask. When she saw Hudson standing there, she pulled her legs quickly to her chest and wrapped her hands around her knees, trying to hide her nakedness. "What are you doing in here? Get out this—"

She paused when she noticed the hair dryer floating next to her, and Katie standing there with murder in her eyes. Mr. Fennimore stood in the doorway, eyes wide and a hand over his mouth, a horrified witness to what had almost happened.

"I thought once I got rid of Randall, Daddy would be all mine again!" Katie screamed at her mother, her face turning red as tears cascaded down her cheeks. "But no, then I had to share him with you. The trips down to the pond without me, all the hours consoling and comforting each other. Daddy's mine, he's mine! And I'll get rid of anybody who gets between us!"

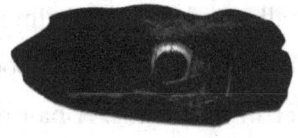

Hudson started down the hill again. The Fennimores were inside, trying to come to grips with what they'd just learned and reach a decision on how best to handle it. He doubted they would contact the authorities and report the truth of Randall's death, but at the very least Katie was in for years of serious therapy. He didn't know how Mr. and Mrs. Fennimore would ever sleep easy in the same house with the girl again, but that wasn't his problem. What happened now was up to the family, and Hudson wasn't all that interested. They'd paid him his fee, and that was where his curiosity ended.

After he checked one final thing.

Standing next to the pond, his eyes scanned the icy surface and saw no sign of Randall's spirit, and Hudson doubted it would return. The boy's work here was done.

As was Hudson's.

DOOR TO DOOR

Becca opened the door to find a thin young man in an oversized suit sweating on her doorstep, a briefcase clutched by his leg. "Hello, ma'am, and how are you this fine morning?"

Becca sighed. She wasn't in the mood for a door-to-door salesman, she had a sink full of dishes waiting to be washed. "I'm fine, but I'm terribly busy."

"I understand that, ma'am, and I promise not to take up too much of your time. Just answer me one question: do you currently have a belief system in your life?"

Becca was already in the process of closing the door in the young man's face, but she paused. "Well, um, actually no. The last one I had fell apart just recently and I haven't had time to go shopping for a new one."

"Well, now you don't have to. I'm bringing one directly to you."

"I don't know, I'm very picky about my belief systems, and most of the ones I've seen advertised recently just don't have all the components I'm looking for."

"Not to worry," the young man said with a megawatt smile. "I'm not offering any pre-packaged belief system here. Instead, I have a variety of components and elements that you can pick and choose from to create your very own."

Becca raised her eyebrows. "Really?"

"Really." Here the young man held up the briefcase so Becca could read the words on the front: "DO-IT-YOUR-SELF RELIGION".

She chewed on her lower lip for a moment, considering the dishes and the other errands that needed to be done. Finally she said, "You can come in, but we have to make this quick."

"Of course."

She showed the young man to the living room, where he sat on the sofa, placing the briefcase before him on the coffee table. "Okay, ma'am, let's get started. Tell me, what do you consider the most important aspect of a belief system?"

"An afterlife," Becca said without hesitation. "It's just too depressing to think that this life is all we get, and that suffering has no ultimate reward. Got to have an afterlife."

The young man opened the briefcase and pulled out several pamphlets, fanning them across the table. "We have a variety of afterlives to choose from. There's your standard street-of-gold Paradise, the living-your-fondest-dream-for-eternity package, the classic angels-on-clouds-with-harps, and this month we're running a special on Heaven-on-Earth."

Becca thought it over for a moment. "I think I like the living-your-fondest-dream one."

"Excellent choice. Now—"

"But no Hell," she interjected.

"No Hell?"

She shook her head. "The whole idea of being subjected to eternal torment just because you don't conform *exactly* to some unknowable deity's code of conduct is rather distasteful. So, no Hell for me, thank you very much."

"Very well," the young man said, putting away all the pamphlets but one. "Now, would you like your belief system to be based on the Golden Rule, as most are?"

"I suppose…but let's not get overly zealous with it."

"Meaning?"

"Well, I'm all for being kind and fair and all that, but I'm not a total turn-the-other-cheeker. Retribution is perfectly acceptable when you've been grossly wronged in some way."

"Ah, so you want the Golden Rule with a little eye-for-an-eye thrown in."

"Exactly."

Another pamphlet was placed on the table. "Do you want a personified god, or something a little more general and vague, like nature or the ever-popular god-is-in-all-of-us?"

"Could I have a woman god?"

"You can have anything you want."

"Okay then, I want a woman god. Strong, regal, an Amazon-type that doesn't take shit from anyone."

"One bitch-goddess coming up," the young man said, riffling through the pamphlets in his case until he found the right one. "Murder?"

"Only in cases of self-defense or capital punishment."

"Contraception? Abortion?"

"Yes to both. I'm a feminist, after all."

"Races equal?"

Only a slight pause. "Sure, I'm a progressive kind of gal."

"Homosexuals?"

A longer pause. "Well, I guess they're okay as long as they don't talk about it too much."

"Let's see what I have that might—"

"No, no, on second thought, I'm going to take a pass on homosexuals. I mean, they're not as bad as pedophiles or rapists, but still…"

The young man nodded. "Gotcha."

"I don't suppose…"

The young man leaned forward. "What is it, ma'am?

Feel free to ask for exactly what you want."

"Well, I was just thinking…would it be possible to get a belief system where certain behaviors are unacceptable for everyone *but* me?"

"What type of behaviors?"

Becca blushed, fiddled with the hem of her skirt, then said, "Well, of course I believe that married couples should be faithful to one another, but hypothetically if one's husband was overly neglectful and a woman felt her needs weren't being met…"

"Say no more," the young man said, placing a few more pamphlets on the table.

"Delightful," Becca said, clapping her hands.

"Well, I think we have the beginnings of a strong personal belief system here. I'll leave a questionnaire with you to hammer out some of the smaller details, like views on envy, greed, pride. And now I need you to sign this contract and we'll be all set."

Becca took the proffered piece of paper, looking it over. "What is all this going to cost me?"

The young man said nothing for a moment, the left corner of his mouth lifting in a curlicue of a smile. "Why, just your soul, of course."

"Sounds reasonable," Becca said, and signed.

SANTA'S LITTLE SPY

"Goodness, look at the time," Carol said. "I should probably be getting home."

Fran took another sip of wine, then glanced at the clock. "Oh, I had no idea it was so late. I know a certain little girl who is up past her bedtime."

Fran's six-year-old daughter, Beth, was on the floor by the Christmas tree, playing some game on the iPad that Fran herself found incomprehensible. She looked up at her mother's words, defiance already in her eyes. She resembled her father so much in moments of belligerence. "Mom, can't I stay up a little longer? It's not a school night or nothing."

"Or *anything*. And you don't want to argue with me, do you? Remember, Santa has his little spy watching you."

Beth gasped, her eyes immediately shooting to the

mantel. "Okay, Mommy, I'm going to bed right now."

"Get into your pjs and brush your teeth, and I'll be up to say goodnight in just a few minutes."

Beth climbed up on the sofa, first gave Fran a peck on the cheek, and then Carol. Then she bounded back to the floor and started toward the stairs. Halfway there she paused and scurried back to the fireplace, staring up at the elf perched on the far-right edge of the mantel. "Goodnight, Paul. I'll come find you in the morning."

Then the girl was out of the room and up the stairs in a blur.

"Well, that was easy," Carol said.

Fran sank back into the cushions and pointed to the mantel. "Whoever invented the Elf on the Shelf is a genius. Beth thinks it watches her every move and reports back to Santa, which means at least for one month of the year she's very complaint. When Paul bought the thing last year, I thought he was crazy, but I have to admit it really works."

"Yeah, sounds great." Carol swirled her wine around in the glass, staring at the little whirlpool it made.

Fran scrutinized the other woman for a moment in silence, then said, "What's up, Carol?"

"Nothing, it's just late and I'm tired."

"Don't bullshit me. We've been best friends since the tenth grade, and I know when something's on your mind. Spill it."

"It's just…well, don't you find it the least bit creepy that Beth named her elf after her dead father?"

Fran considered the question and shrugged with one shoulder. "At first, but I guess it makes sense in a strange way. I mean, Paul passed only a couple of months ago. Beth is still trying to process it. Hell, *I'm* still trying to process it."

Carol reached out, took one of Fran's hands and squeezed it. "I'm sorry, I shouldn't have even brought it up."

"It's okay. I'm coping, really. With the help of good friends and massive amounts of wine." With that, Fran drained her glass.

Carol laughed softly and followed suit. "I really do need to go. I'm exhausted."

"And you've had three glasses of wine. Maybe it's not such a good idea for you to be driving all the way across town."

"You offering to put me up for the night?"

"You know what they say about *me casa*."

"You're too kind. I really should be embarrassed—this is the third time in the last month I've overindulged and had to crash here. It's like I'm turning into an old lush."

"Well," Fran said with a pointed stare, "to an outside observer, it might seem you were doing it on purpose just to keep a grieving widow company."

Carol laughed but didn't answer. Instead, she gathered up the two wine glasses and the empty bottle.

"Leave the cleanup for the morning," Fran said with a

flip of her hand. "I can barely keep my eyes open. Let's head on up, I'll tuck Beth in, then we can crash."

"Sounds like a plan to me."

They had just started up the stairs when Carol suddenly stopped. "What about the elf?"

"What?" Fran said, turning back to her friend.

"The elf...aren't you supposed to move it around every night so Beth finds it in a different location each morning?"

Fran groaned and walked back across the living room. She picked up the elf and moved it from the right side of the mantel to the left.

"Well, that was certainly creative," Carol said when her friend rejoined her on the stairs.

"It's too late to be creative. I'll just tell her little Paul was too tired to do any extensive traveling."

Fran was awakened the next morning by a continuous prodding in her shoulder and a high-pitched voice repeating, "Mommy, get up," over and over. She tried to ignore it, but when it became apparent Beth would not be dissuaded, Fran finally pried her eyes open. She had pulled the curtains the night before, but white-hot sunlight leaked in around the edges, stinging her eyes.

"Beth, please stop poking me," she croaked. "It's too early for this."

But was it? The sunlight suggested not. Raising herself on a forearm, she squinted at the clock on the bedside table. 10:25. Damn, much later than she thought. Not that it mattered, Beth was out of school for Christmas vacation.

"Carol?" Fran said, but when she turned she found the other side of the bed vacated. Of course, Carol had a job and Fran vaguely remembered hearing the alarm on the other woman's phone going off early this morning.

"Mommy, you gonna get up? I've been up *forever*."

Fran yawned and arched her back. "You need me to fix you some breakfast?"

"I already made cereal."

Fran groaned. If Beth had made her own breakfast, that meant the kitchen was going to be a disaster area.

"Mommy, please get up. I need you to help me find Paul."

"What?"

"I can't find Paul and I've looked everywhere."

Another groan. "Honey, you can't have looked everywhere."

"But I did. I even looked in your room."

This brought Fran instantly to full wakefulness, and she sat up in bed, scanning her room. All the drawers of her dresser were opened, and clothes were scattered across the floor. "Beth, I've told you never to go through Mommy's things. Santa is not going to be happy about this."

"But I've got to find Paul," Beth whined. "He's missing."

"He's not missing. In fact, he's probably not far from where he was last night."

"He's not, Mommy. What if someone kidnapped him?"

"Okay, okay, you win. I'll help you look."

Throwing back the covers, Fran swung her feet onto the floor, pausing for a moment before heaving herself to a standing position, wobbling slightly before getting her balance. Her mouth tasted foul, like some small animal had crawled in there, taken a crap, then died. She wanted to go scrub her teeth and gargle mouthwash for about twenty minutes, but Beth already had one of her hands and was tugging her toward the hallway.

Fran paused at the top of the stairs, remembering standing here two months prior, looking down to the first floor and seeing Paul sprawled on the landing, his head twisted at an impossible angle. Beth had been at school at the time, so luckily had been spared the sight of her father's body. All she knew was that he'd had an accident and had gone to be with God.

At least Paul's life insurance had left them financially

secure. Fran didn't even have to rush to find a job, at least not for a little while.

Beth was still tugging at Fran's hand. "Hurry, Mommy, hurry! We have to find Paul!"

"Calm down," Fran said, following her daughter down the stairs. "I'm telling you, Paul is probably—"

Fran stopped speaking mid-sentence as she and Beth walked into the living room. Her eyes fell on the mantel, zeroing in on the left end where she'd placed the elf last night. Only now it wasn't there.

Beth had let go of her hand and run over to the sofa, getting down on her hands and knees, and peering underneath it. Fran walked over to the fireplace and looked around on the floor, assuming the elf must have fallen off the mantel, but the thing was nowhere to be seen. But that was impossible. She may have had a bit too much wine last night but she distinctly remembered moving the elf from one end of the mantel to the other. Carol had even said—

Carol. Of course. She must have moved the elf before she left this morning.

Beth was now on the sofa, digging down between the cushions. "Help me look, Mommy."

"Mommy's starving, so I'm going to go get a bite of breakfast, then I'll help you ransack the place on one condition. You have to help me clean up once we find the elf. Deal?"

"Okay, Mommy."

117

Fran walked into the kitchen, which was indeed a disaster area. Beth had dragged a chair over to the countertop, apparently climbing up to get the cereal from the cabinet, in the process knocking over the salt and pepper shakers and a box of toothpicks, scattering them everywhere. Fruity Pebbles were also scattered all over the place, and the opened carton of milk was still sitting on the floor in front of the refrigerator, which was ajar.

Picking up the milk, Fran stowed it in the fridge, popped open the freezer and snagged a couple of frozen waffles, then walked over to the microwave. She pressed the button to open the microwave—

—and gasped.

There was the elf, sitting in the microwave.

Grinning at her.

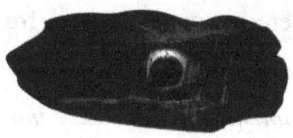

Three days later, Fran got up early—earlier than she had in quite some time. She peeked into Beth's room, finding the girl snuggled under the covers and snoring softly, then made her way downstairs.

After tucking Beth in the previous night, Fran had placed the elf at the very back of the top shelf in the hall closet, behind a stack of photo albums. She didn't even have to go to the closet now to check, because as she came down into the living room, she saw the damn thing perched on the coffee table.

She froze where she was, feeling as if her entire body had been dunked in a vat of ice water. This was the fourth day in a row that the elf had ended up in a different spot from the one in which she'd left it, starting with the infamous microwave discovery. That first day she'd assumed Carol had moved it, but her friend said no, and Carol hadn't stayed the night again since. Which only left Beth.

As if on cue, Fran heard little feet pounding down the stairs behind her. "Paul!" Beth squealed, running past her mother and jumping up and down in front of the elf.

"Beth, how long have you been awake?"

"I just woke up a minute ago when you were closing my bedroom door."

Fran knelt down so she and her daughter were eye to eye. "Did you get up some time last night after Mommy went to bed?"

"No, Mommy."

"Don't lie," Fran said, grabbing her daughter by the shoulders.

"I'm not lying, cross my heart. Will you make me and Paul some breakfast?"

Letting her hands fall away from Beth, Fran sighed.

"Sure. Give me just a minute and I'll go fix some pancakes."

Beth started toward the kitchen. "Will you put blueberries in them? Blueberry pancakes are Paul's favorite."

Another of those ice-water chills spread over every inch of Fran's skin. Blueberry pancakes had been her late husband's favorite. Beth had named the elf after her father, and was now attributing some of Paul's traits to it. Did that mean the girl was actually pretending the elf *was* her father? And did that have something to do with why Beth was moving the thing around at night?

And it had to be Beth, there was no other possible explanation. Although—

Fran walked down the short hallway that led to the laundry room then the garage, stopping at the closet. Opening the door, she stood on her tiptoes and stared at the top shelf. The photo albums were still there, stacked neatly in what appeared to be the same position they'd been last night. In fact, nothing seemed disturbed or out of place.

How would Beth have even known where to look? And there was the question of how she could have possibly reached the elf back there? Even if she'd gotten the step ladder, it still wouldn't have been high enough. She didn't see how her daughter could have possibly taken the elf from the shelf.

But what alternative did that leave?

She could hear Beth giggling and she made her way slowly back to the living room. Beth had come back from the kitchen, now kneeling in front of the coffee table. Her head was turned and leaned close to the elf, almost as if the thing were whispering in her ear. A joke, judging by her trilling laughter.

"Beth, honey, what are you doing?"

"Nothing, Mommy. Paul was just telling me a story."

"What kind of a story?"

"It's about a princess who gets kidnapped by an evil witch, but the two become best friends and go on all kinds of adventures together."

Fran actually stopped breathing for a few seconds. "Beth, have you been in your daddy's office? Tell me the truth now."

"No, Mommy. I haven't been in there since Daddy went to be with God."

Of course she hadn't. Fran had kept Paul's office locked up since then, even she hadn't been in there. So how could Beth know about—

"Mommy," Beth said. "Paul wants to know when you're going to make those blueberry pancakes."

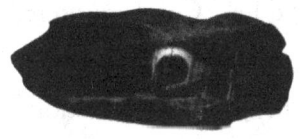

"What are you saying?" Carol asked.

Fran was sitting in the living room, her phone pressed against the side of her face. Beth was upstairs in her room, asleep. "I'm saying that there's no way Beth could have known about the book."

"I thought you and Paul had read all of his books to her."

"I'm not talking about one of his published books. This was a new one, the one he was working on when he died. *The Princess and the Witch*, he let me read the first few chapters, but no one else had seen it, not even his editor. So Beth couldn't have known about it. Yet she described the plot to me, said the elf told it to her."

Silence from the other end of the phone. Then, "I'm still not sure what you're suggesting."

"Hell, I don't know what I'm suggesting either. I'm just trying to figure this out."

"Well…did it ever occur to you that maybe Paul was telling the story to Beth as he was writing it, sort of like a bedtime story or something?"

"I suppose that's possible, but why wouldn't he have mentioned that to me?"

"Why would he?" Carol countered.

Fran paused, considering. "I guess he might not have thought it important enough to mention."

"And as for Beth somehow getting the elf out of the hall closet, aren't you always telling me how she manages to get the stuff out of the high cabinets in the kitchen?"

"Yes, but that's different. She drags over a chair and climbs from there onto the countertops. There was nothing around for her to climb on to get up to that shelf in the closet."

"Maybe she dragged a chair over then put it back."

"Beth has never been one for putting things back where she found them. And why would she be doing this anyway, moving the elf around?"

"It's like you said, she's trying to process the loss of her father. I'd be surprised if she wasn't acting a little strangely. If you're really worried about it, though, make an appointment with a child psychologist."

"Maybe."

"Might not be a bad idea for yourself, for that matter."

Fran laughed softly. "What, are you saying I'm crazy?"

"Nutty as a fruitcake."

"I certainly feel like I'm losing my mind. I mean, with the doll seeming to move around on its own, it's like I'm in *Trilogy of Terror* or something."

"Do you want me to come over?"

Fran thought about it, almost said yes, but finally said, "No, don't be silly. It's too late for you to be driving across town."

"I don't mind, really. Just say the word, and I'm there."

"I'm fine. Paul's death...well, I guess it has messed

with my head more than I've wanted to admit."

"Okay, but if you need anything, anything at all, just call me."

"Will do. Thanks for everything, Carol. I love you."

"Love you too, fruitcake."

Fran laughed and hung up the phone. She got up and started for the stairs, pausing when she spotted the elf sitting on an end table. Snatching it up, she went into the kitchen and used the foot pedal to pop open the lid on the trashcan. She moved aside a milk jug, coffee grounds, a pizza box, then tossed the elf inside, covering it back over as if burying the thing.

"Good riddance," she said, letting the lid bang shut.

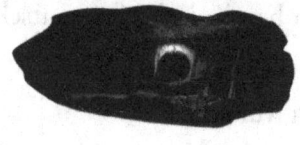

The next morning, Fran came awake to the feel of her hair being pulled. Not hard enough to hurt, just enough to be annoying. "Beth, stop that."

Another tug and Fran rolled over and opened her eyes—

—and screamed.

The elf was sitting on the pillow next to her head, its painted-on smile mocking and cruel. Some old spaghetti was stuck to the side of its face. Fran swatted at the thing, sending it sailing off the bed and onto the floor. She climbed out of the bed on the opposite side, walking cautiously around until she could see the elf lying on the carpet. On its back, arms splayed out crucifixion style, one leg over the other, the head twisted to the right. Something about the elf's positioning troubled Fran, needling at her, but she couldn't quite—

Paul. That was the same position his body had been in at the foot of the stairs after his fall. Exactly the same.

Stiffening her resolve, Fran snatched up the doll and hurried to Beth's bedroom. The girl was in bed with her eyes closed, playing possum, Fran was sure. She stood there for a moment and when Beth persisted with the pretense of sleep, Fran said loudly, "Beth!"

The girl started, then sat up, rubbing her eyes. "Good morning, Mommy."

"Beth, this has got to stop." Fran held up the elf, dangling from her hand by the feet.

"Paul!" Beth squealed. "Mommy, you're not supposed to touch him, it takes his magic away."

Fran began violently shaking the doll. "I don't know if you think this is funny or what, but I'm not amused, and I'm telling you *right now* I'm not going to stand for it anymore."

"Mommy, please stop, you're hurting him!"

Fran threw the elf to the floor and stomped on it, hearing a *crack*! When she lifted her foot, she saw a zigzagging line running across its face like a scar. Beth shrieked as if she'd just been scalded and jumped out of bed, running toward the elf. Fran snatched it back up before the girl could grab it.

"Give him to me!" the girl said.

"Now, you shouldn't talk to your mother in that tone. Christmas is only two days away. Santa might just not leave you anything."

"I don't care. Santa Claus isn't even real. Paul told me so."

"Did he now? What else did he tell you?"

"He said you were mean. I told him that wasn't so, but he was right. You are mean!"

With her free hand, Fran smacked Beth in the face. Not with any great force, but it still brought the girl to tears. "This little rebellious phase of yours is over, young lady. Do I make myself clear?"

At first, Beth didn't say anything, just stared up at her mother with a poisonous glare, then she said softly, "You are mean."

Fran waved the elf around in the air. "Say goodbye to your little friend, because this is the last time you're ever going to see him."

And with that, Fran left the room, slamming the door behind her.

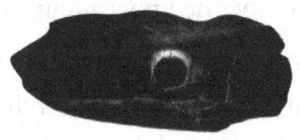

The next morning, Fran was only mildly surprised when she opened the freezer and found the elf sitting in there. She'd almost been expecting something like this, even though yesterday she'd locked the elf away in Paul's old office and slept with the key under her pillow.

"It would appear that Paul found his way out again," Fran said as she walked into the living room.

Beth didn't look up from the iPad. "Paul says you're a bad person, and bad people always get what's coming to them."

"Paul understands the concept of karma, does he?"

Beth didn't respond.

With a sigh, Fran sat cross-legged on the floor next to her daughter. "What do you say we call a truce, huh? I'll stop being mean to you if you stop being mean to me. I mean, I'm not so bad, am I? Daddy left us, but Mommy is still taking care of you, isn't she?"

"You're taking care of me with the money from Daddy's life insurance, so in a way it's Daddy that's still taking care of me."

Fran sat rigidly for a moment. "Did Paul tell you that?"

"Yes."

"Well, what does he know about it?"

Beth looked up and met her mother's eyes, an unwavering gaze that would have been unnerving in an adult but was especially discombobulating in a six year old. "He knows a lot about it."

Then Beth stood up and left the room. Her posture and gait were so much like her father's that it gave Fran chills.

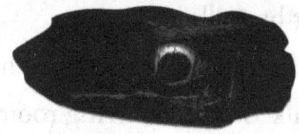

Fran sat on the sofa with a glass of wine, staring across the room at the elf on the mantel. The only light in the room came from the flames crackling in the fireplace and the blinking lights on the Christmas tree in the corner.

It was after ten, Beth had been in bed for almost two hours. Locked in her room. Fran wasn't exactly the handiest woman in the world, but she'd managed to install the padlock on the outside of the door. No chance Beth was going to get out tonight. It was just Fran...and Paul.

In the flickering light, the elf's cracked face resembled an imp of the devil. Which made sense in a way. Rearrange the letters in Santa, and you get Satan. Had to be more than a coincidence.

Fran glanced at the tree. She had yet to retrieve Beth's

gifts from the attic and put them out for the girl to find in the morning. And Fran thought she might not bother. Beth had, after all, been a very naughty girl. Saint Nick might just have to pass her by this year.

Placing the wine glass on the coffee table, Fran stood and walked to the mantel. She stared at the elf for a few moments, as if daring it to…well, she didn't know what. Move, speak, stand and do a little tap dance routine. Laughing at her own foolishness, she reached out and flicked the elf with a finger.

"So Beth seems to think you're her father," Fran said. "Not surprising, I suppose. You were her hero. I mean, I'm the one that took care of her, fed her, planned all her birthday parties, helped her with her homework, but still she looked up to you as if you were a god. What did you ever do for her? Read her bedtime stories? Big deal. You could barely even support us, which is why we were about to lose the house. Always writing those stupid children's books, but you were no good. You couldn't accept that you were never going to make it big, wouldn't just give up the stupid writing dream and get a real job. About all you had to offer was the life insurance, a hell of a policy indeed."

Fran paused, reached out and picked up the elf, pulling it in close to her face. "I got rid of you once, I can do it again." And with that, she casually tossed the thing into the fire, then went upstairs.

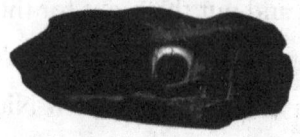

It was the stinging smell of smoke and charred plastic in her nostrils that roused Fran from sleep. She groped for the bedside lamp and finally found the switch. She barely stifled a yelp when she saw Beth standing at the foot of the bed.

"How did you get out of your room?" Fran asked, her mind still groggy.

"Paul let me out."

"What are you talking about? What's going on?"

"Paul says you shouldn't have pushed him. It wasn't very nice. Paul says you're a bad girl, and bad girls get punished."

Fran was about to respond when she noticed the smoke leaking into her room from the hallway. "Oh my god, where's that coming from?"

Beth remained still, her expression blank, her eyes dead. "Paul caught some stuff on fire in the living room before he came up to let me out of my room. It wasn't his fault though. *Someone* threw him in the fireplace."

The brain fog finally dissipated and Fran was out of bed in a flash, rushing past her daughter and out into the hallway. Smoke was flowing up the stairs, burning her lungs and sending her into a coughing fit. Raising the collar of her nightgown to cover her mouth, she headed for the stairs. She spotted the charred elf on the first stair a split second before her foot landed on it. The thing rolled beneath her, causing her foot to fly out from under her. She raised her arms to try to grab the railing, but it was too late. Gravity did its thing and sent her toppling down the stairs, practically somersaulting toward the first floor landing. Her side banged into the edge of a stair and she both felt and heard some of her ribs snap, and she cracked her head against the banister. She threw out an arm to try to stop her fall, but her elbow bent the wrong way and pain exploded up into her shoulder. When she finally crashed to the tiled landing, her head banged into the floor with such force it made her vision gray around the edges.

Her head was turned to the side so that she was facing the living room. The curtains and the sofa were on fire, black smoke filling the air like thunderheads. She tried to sit up but found she couldn't. Panic flared inside her as bright as the fire that was consuming the living room, and she wondered if she'd damaged her spine, rendering her paralyzed. The smoke was filling her lungs, and her body shook with the force of her coughing. She could feel the heat from the flames and she tried to will her arms to move, to drag herself toward the door, but nothing.

Tiny sock-clad feet suddenly stepped into her vision. Her daughter knelt before her and looked down at Fran without any hint of emotion. She carried the burned elf in her arms. Holding the thing up to her ear, she nodded solemnly, then turned her attention back to her mother. "Daddy says Merry Christmas."

Then Beth stood up and walked out of her line of sight. Fran heard the front door open and close. She tried to call out to her daughter but all she could manage was a hoarse rattling. She still could not move, could only lie there helpless, choking on smoke, watching the flames get closer.

BREAKING UP IS HARD TO DO

Hudson leaned back in the comfortable recliner and stared across the coffee table at his new client, waiting for her to speak. She sat on the sofa, wearing a simple cotton dress of powder blue. She was probably in her mid-forties but could have easily passed for twenty-something, her wavy hair colored to a blazing auburn. She was definitely an attractive woman, but Hudson didn't dwell too much on that.

The client, Jessica, looked uncomfortable, chewing on her lower lip and constantly smoothing her skirt over her lap. Since offering Hudson a glass of tea several moments ago, which he had politely refused, she had said nothing. Perhaps she was waiting for him to get the ball rolling, but that wasn't how he worked. If she was serious about contracting Hudson's services, she would have to be willing to make the first move.

133

He didn't have time for games.

"You sure you wouldn't like some tea?" she said suddenly. "It's freshly made."

"Thank you, no," Hudson said, giving her a look as if to say, *Haven't we wasted enough time?*

"I'm sorry, I'm just nervous. I've never done anything like this before."

Hudson remained silent. He supposed he could have said something to ease her discomfort, but that wasn't his job. He wasn't paid to coddle nervous clients and handhold them through the proceedings.

"So how long have you been in this line of work, Mr. Hudson?"

"A while," he said.

"Kind of an unusual job, isn't it?"

"Pays the bills."

"I guess so. I mean, your fee is rather…exorbitant."

"I'm worth it, trust me."

"Oh, I know. My friend Cole swears by you."

"Nice to hear."

Jessica fell back into the arms of silence, taking refuge there. Hudson was becoming impatient; his time was a valuable commodity. He glanced pointedly at his watch, then back at the client.

"So you can really get rid of ghosts?" she said, sounding very much like a child all of a sudden, asking her father to make the monster under her bed go away.

"Among other things, yes."

"What are we talking here? Exorcism?"

"Nothing like that. Ghosts were once people. They are sometimes confused, sometimes angry, often desperate to cling to those things they knew in life, but they still maintain their basic humanity. They can usually be reasoned with."

"Usually?" Jessica raised an eyebrow.

"Well, just like not all people can be reasoned with, neither can all ghosts."

"That's not exactly comforting."

"I'm not one to sugarcoat things."

"Yes, I kind of figured that out already."

"So why don't you tell me about your ghost?"

"Oh, my house isn't haunted."

Hudson frowned, his impatience rapidly turning toward anger. He certainly hoped he hadn't driven out here for nothing. "I'm confused."

"It's my brother's place that's haunted," she explained. "Ty has an apartment down by the beach. A haunted apartment, can you imagine that?"

"I've seen stranger things."

"Yes, I suppose you have. In any case, I was hoping you could get rid of the ghost that haunts my brother's apartment."

"I don't understand, why isn't your brother hiring me

himself?"

Jessica chewed on her lip some more. If she wasn't careful, Hudson thought, she was going to draw blood. Finally she said, "My brother doesn't *want* to get rid of the ghost."

"He doesn't? And why is that?"

"You see, my brother and his lover, Kris, had been together for about five years when Kris died from colon cancer."

"Did he die in the apartment?"

Jessica nodded. "There was nothing the doctors could do, and Kris said he didn't want to spend his last days in a clinical hospital environment. So Ty took him home and cared for him until…well, until the end."

"And now Kris's spirit still inhabits the apartment?"

Jessica nodded again, seeming incapable of speaking. Tears shimmered in her eyes but did not fall.

"How long ago did Kris die?"

"Three years. My brother has been living in that apartment with a dead man for three years now."

"Have you seen the ghost yourself?"

"Yes. He looks real, I mean he looks *whole*. Just looking at him, you'd never guess he was a spirit, but when you try to touch him, your hand passes right through like there's nothing there but air. And when he speaks, his voice is tinny and distant, like he's talking through a bad intercom system. Is that normal?"

"There really is no 'normal' in situations such as these,"

Hudson said with a shrug. "Different spirits manifest themselves in different ways. They're all unique."

"Do you think you can get Kris's spirit to move on or go into the light or whatever?"

"But if your brother doesn't want—"

"It isn't healthy!" Jessica exclaimed, her vehemence surprising Hudson, and by the look on her face, surprising herself. In a calmer voice, she said, "Having Kris's ghost there is preventing Ty from moving on with his life, finding someone new. Except for work, he rarely goes out. He just shuts himself in that apartment with a ghost, pretending things are just as they were, denying the fact that his lover is dead. It just isn't healthy, and I worry about what it's doing to his mental state."

Hudson leaned forward, propping his elbows on his knees. "I appreciate your concern for your brother, but I can't exactly go into a man's home and perform my services if he doesn't want me there."

"Just go and talk to him. He won't listen to me, but you're an expert. You might be able to get through to him. That's all I'm asking, is for you to *try*. I'll pay you regardless of the results."

"I'm still not sure—"

"I'll pay double your usual fee."

"I'll do it," Hudson said immediately. He liked to think of himself as an ethical man, but he was also no fool.

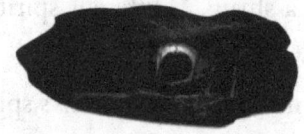

The door was opened seconds after Hudson knocked. Ty stood in the doorway with a half-smile curling one corner of his mouth. He had his sister's eyes and coloring, although the red in his hair appeared to be natural and not from a bottle. "You must be the ghostbuster guy," he said.

"I take it your sister called you."

"Yeah, she told me she was sending you over. I tried to dissuade her, but if you knew my sister, you'd know how futile such an attempt is. Please, come in."

Ty moved aside, and Hudson stepped through the doorway. He found himself in a combination living/dining room, with a small square of a kitchen opening off of it. A stub of a hallway branched off to the right, two closed doorways at its end. The bedroom and bathroom, Hudson assumed. There were glass patio doors that opened onto a balcony that contained a small bistro set of black iron and a gas grill; there was a breathtaking view of the beach from the balcony. The apartment was small but tidy.

"Funny," Ty said, "you don't look anything like Bill Murray."

"My name is Hudson."

"I'm Ty, but you already know that."

Hudson nodded and shook Ty's hand. "I suppose you know why I'm here."

"My sister thinks I'm wasting away in here with my phantom lover," Ty said, placing the back of a hand against his forehead like a character in some melodramatic film.

"That's about the long and short of it."

"I love Jess to death, but sometimes she can be a bit unbearable."

"She's just worried about you."

"Well, I'm thirty-eight years old. A little old to need babysitting. Then again, I guess to her I'll always be her baby brother."

Hudson tried a polite laugh on for size but found it an ill fit. Ty had been nothing but welcoming, but Hudson had a sixth sense that told him when he wasn't wanted, and this was one of those times. Still, he planned to earn his paycheck. "I'm just here to talk with you, that's all. Maybe you even have some questions for me."

"Not really, but I'll humor my sister and talk to you for a bit. Have a seat, I'll bring us some tea."

Hudson took a seat in a wicker rocker while Ty went into the kitchen, returning a moment later with two glasses of iced tea. Hudson took a sip, found it a bit too sugary for his tastes, and sat it down on a cork-board coaster. "Is your lover in the apartment now?"

Ty smiled at him. "A man who gets right to the point.

I admire that. To answer your question, Kris is pretty much *always* in the apartment, but I suspect you already know how that works."

"Yes, but I wasn't sure if you did."

"No offense, Mr. Hudson, but I've been living with this for three years now. I know you're some kind of ghost authority, but I'm not a complete moron on the subject myself."

"Didn't mean to imply that you were."

Ty took a seat on a gold-upholstered divan and took a long swallow of his tea. "So, what exactly did my sister tell you? That she thinks I'm going crazy?"

"In so many words, yes." Hudson saw no reason to shy away from the truth. "She says you've pretty much isolated yourself in the apartment and refuse to accept the reality of the situation."

"And which reality would that be?"

"That your lover is dead."

Ty's face become suddenly grim, his mouth shriveling as if he'd tasted something sour, and his eyes, which had formerly been so warm, turned into blue chips of ice. "I'm very much aware that Kris is dead. I'm the one who stayed by his side while he wasted away. I'm the one who listened to him cry and tried to comfort him when the pain got so bad that even the morphine wasn't enough to soothe it. I'm the one who held his hand as he breathed his last breath. Believe me, I had no choice but to accept that reality."

"I didn't mean any offense. I was simply repeating what your sister told me."

The ice began to melt and some of the warmth returned to Ty's eyes. "I'm sorry, I don't mean to take it out on you. I know you're just trying to help, as is Jess. She just doesn't understand."

"Understand what?"

"Mr. Hudson, I assure you that my life isn't in some kind limbo. I have a thriving career. I have a great group of friends, and contrary to what my sister may believe, I spend time with them quite often. I would spend more time with Jess if she would back off and stop trying to convince me that my relationship with Kris is unhealthy."

Hudson glanced at his glass of tea and considered taking another sip just to be polite, but then decided against it. "When you say 'relationship…'"

"Well, if we're going to be talking about Kris, it's only right that he be present to take part in the conversation. Kris, sweetie, why don't you come on out."

And just like that, Kris was there. One minute he wasn't, the next he was standing beside the divan. He was tall with a thick head of midnight black hair, eyes the green of a summer field, and an easy smile. Hudson had been telling the truth when he told Jessica that different spirits manifested themselves in different ways. Some were insubstantial wraiths, in human form but transparent. Some appeared as a mist or a shadow. Some were invisible to the eye. And then some, like Kris, were fully realized. The ghost looked to be solid, perfectly three-dimensional, although Hudson had no doubt Jessica's assertion that you could reach right through him was correct. No matter what the appearance, ghosts had no substance, no physical matter.

"Kris," Ty said, "this is Hudson, the ghostbuster guy Jess hired."

Amusement crinkled the corners of Kris's eyes. "Nice to meet you." His voice sounded hollow and as if it were coming from a great distance, almost as if he were speaking from the bottom of a deep well.

Ty stared up at the ghost for a moment, his eyes shining with something Hudson assumed was love, though he had little experience with it himself. Then Ty turned back to Hudson and said, almost as if he had been privy to the man's thoughts, "Have you ever been in love, Mr. Hudson?"

"I really don't see what my personal life has to do with anything," Hudson said, not unkindly but matter-of-factly. The fact was, he had no personal life, and he liked it that way. Relationships and sex had never held much interest for him.

"Fair enough. Until I met Kris eight years ago, I'd never been in love. I'm not sure I even believed in love. Oh, I'd been in lust, and I'd been in a few committed relationships, but I had never really been head-over-heels, arrow-through-the-heart in love. Then I met Kris, and all that changed. Not right away. At first he was just a cute guy I wanted to sleep with, but then after I finally got him in my bed, I found I didn't want to kick him out. We started dating, and after six months I couldn't imagine having anyone other than Kris in my life. That was unusual for me. Typically after six months, I was tired of a guy and ready to move on. With Kris, it was different. He was all I wanted."

Hudson shifted his weight as if uncomfortable in the chair. In truth, what he was uncomfortable with was this story. Hudson cared little about the lives of his clients, and he found himself growing bored the more Ty talked.

Ty seemed to sense this. Hudson had to hand it to the man; he could certainly read people. "I'm sorry if this is a case of too much information, Mr. Hudson, but you've been hired by my sister to convince me that my continued relationship with Kris is unhealthy. All I ask is for you to allow me the leeway of stating my case."

Feeling somewhat chastised, Hudson mumbled an apology.

"For five years, Kris and I lived together in this apartment. Oh, it wasn't all good times. There were arguments, conflicts. Hell, there was one period about a year and a half into the relationship when I thought we were going to break up. But we didn't. We worked through it, and we grew stronger. It wasn't love the way the movies portray it, but it was real, and I was grateful to have found it."

"And I felt the same," Kris said in his faraway voice. "I had been hurt in the past, to the point where I felt that love wasn't worth it. I had resigned myself to living alone for the rest of my life, convincing myself that I actually preferred it, when I met Ty. I was reluctant to get involved at first, but eventually Ty got me to put my past where it belonged...in the past."

Ty took a deep breath, started to speak, stopped, stared down at his hands, and started again. "When Kris died...I don't even know how to describe what I was feeling. It was beyond grief, beyond mourning. I felt a little mad, like perhaps I'd lost my sanity along with my lover. It seemed so cruel, to finally find someone so special only to have him taken away after such a short time. I had never believed in God, but I started to think that I was wrong. Maybe there was a God, but he was less of a benign Father and more a mean-spirited prankster."

When Ty paused again, Hudson asked, "How long after Kris died did his ghost first manifest itself?"

"About a week," Ty said then looked up at Kris. "That sound right?"

"Yes, about that. I clearly remembered the pain of my illness, and I knew I was dead. But suddenly I was here as well. I don't know how or why, but I honestly haven't spent too much time trying to figure it out. I'm here, in some form, and that's good enough for me."

Ty laughed. "I was a little afraid when I first saw him. I guess years of ghost stories and haunted house movies had brainwashed me into thinking Kris was some kind of evil specter. But then he started talking to me, and I realized it was just Kris. He was still with me, even after death. I was so ecstatic. I haven't wasted any time trying to analyze it, I'm just so overjoyed to be reunited with him."

Turning his attention to the ghost, Hudson said, "But don't you feel the *pull*? Most spirits I've been in contact with say they feel some pull to the other side—whatever that might be—and they have to actively fight it in order to stay on the mortal plane."

"Sure, I feel it, but it's not as insistent as you might imagine. It's not like a tether trying to yank me away; it's more like a gentle tugging at my shirttail. A minor annoyance at best, not difficult at all to resist."

"But why resist it at all? It's the natural order of things, the next step."

"I don't plan to resist for eternity. Just until the two of us can take that next step together. Whatever grand adventure awaits us after this world, we'll undertake it together."

"And until then?"

"Until then we're a couple," Ty said. "An unconventional one, I'll grant you, but we were already unconventional before Kris died. The thing is, while Kris is dead, he isn't *gone*. He's still here, all the things that make him the man I love are still present, so why would I want to find anyone else? My sister wants me to move on with my life, but to her that means turning my back on the only man I've ever wanted to share my life with. I don't have to move on with my life, because my life is here with Kris."

Hudson sat in silence for a moment, staring from one man to the other, from the man to the spirit. They both spoke with conviction, and Hudson had to admit that Ty seemed neither unhappy nor mentally unstable. He was a man in love, and there was always a bit of foolishness and madness that came along with that, but he didn't seem like someone about whom his sister needed to worry. Still, Hudson thought he'd give it one more shot.

"If you'll excuse me for getting so personal, but what about…sex?"

"What about it?" Ty asked with a smile.

"Do you not find it frustrating that the two of you cannot be physically intimate?"

"I'm beyond the need for sex," Kris said. "And Ty, well, let's just say he takes care of himself."

"While you whisper some of the nastiest things I've ever heard in my ear."

Shifting uncomfortably again, Hudson said, "And that's enough for you?"

Ty fixed Hudson with a candid stare and said, "Truth be told, Mr. Hudson, sex was never the primary foundation of our relationship. I'm not going to say that we didn't have an amazing sex life before Kris died, because we did, but that wasn't what we loved most about one another, it wasn't what kept us together. Do I ever miss sex with Kris? Of course. Do I think our relationship can survive without it? Absolutely."

"But your sister—"

"Let me explain something to you about my sister. I came out to her when I was nineteen, and she didn't understand. She thought I was a freak, and she feared I was going to be miserable for the rest of my life. It took her almost ten years to come around and realize that she'd been wrong. She'll eventually come around about this, too. It may take her awhile, but she'll eventually see that I'm happy. Until then, it's just a waiting game."

Hudson nodded and stood, the rocker creaking as he removed the bulk of his weight from it. "Well, I want to thank you two for your time."

"Leaving already?" Kris said.

"You barely put up a fight," Ty added.

"I don't think there's anything I can tell you that you don't already know. As you said earlier, you're not a moron on the subject of ghosts. You strike me as an intelligent man who has thought this thing through from every possible angle, and you're confident that the course of action you've taken is the right one. There's really nothing more to say. I do apologize if I've wasted your time—"

"Oh, not at all." Ty rose to see Hudson to the door. "I rather enjoyed talking with you, although I think I did most of the talking."

Hudson nodded at the ghost as he passed, and Kris nodded back. At the door, Ty laid a hand on Hudson's arm and said, "Tell my sister I'm okay."

"Will do."

Hudson left the apartment complex, ignoring the beautiful day and the lure of the waves pounding on the beach nearby, intent only on collecting his payment.

"Are you crazy?" Jessica said. They were standing in the living room, Jessica wearing a pair of pleated shorts and a simple cream-colored blouse that showed off her body nicely.

"Is it crazy to expect payment at the end of a job?" Hudson asked.

"But you didn't *do* anything. My brother is still holed up in there with that ghost. What do you expect me to pay you *for*?"

"You did not hire me to get rid of the ghost. You hired me to go talk to your brother, to try to convince him that he needed to move on by getting Kris's ghost to do the same. I did that."

"I talked to my brother. He said you asked a few questions and that was it, that you mostly listened to him and looked pained. That was the word he used, 'pained.'"

"I ascertained that your brother knew exactly what he was doing and that he had no regrets. You want your brother to be happy, to have a fulfilling life. I tell you, he has that already."

"That's impossible. How can he have a fulfilling life with a ghoul, with a memory? I thought you were going to argue, get Ty to see reason, convince him. Instead, he ended up convincing you. I won't pay. You did nothing, and I won't pay."

Hudson's expression remained calm, a tightening around his mouth the only outward sign of his mounting anger. "I'll remind you, you said you would pay 'regardless of the results'. I really am going to insist you pay me for my services."

Jessica laughed, and her eyes squinted in a way that made her face much less beautiful. "And what will you do if I don't? Take me to court? Yours isn't exactly a licensed profession, and I never signed any kind of contract. Legally speaking, I don't think you have a leg to stand on, Mr. Hudson."

Hudson's nostrils flared, just once, but that was enough to make Jessica step back. Hudson rarely lost his temper, but money was the one thing that could set him off, and there was a scent on the air like electricity before a thunderstorm.

When Hudson spoke, his voice was hushed but heated. "You believe I can get rid of ghosts, I know you do. And I can, but that's not all I can do. I can also summon them." When Jessica's eyes widened in fear, Hudson smiled. "That's right, just by speaking a few choice words and performing a simple ritual, I can call any number of spirits to this home. And they will remain bound here until such time as I see fit to release them. And not gentle spirits like Kris, but spirits that are full of rage and hostility toward the living. Is that what you want?"

Jessica tried to speak, managing only a thin whining, so she shook her head in answer.

"Then I suggest you write me a check or you just might find you have a couple dozen unwanted houseguests that won't leave."

Without a word, but with a sense of urgency in every movement, Jessica hurried to her purse and pulled out her checkbook. As she began to scribble furiously, Hudson said, "Don't forget you promised to pay double my usual fee."

Hudson left Jessica's house with the check tucked away in his wallet, laughing to himself. He could no more summon ghosts than he could make it rain on a cloudless day, but Jessica didn't know that. Hudson headed directly to the bank so he could cash the check before the woman changed her mind and tried to cancel it.

No one stiffed Hudson.

THE END OF HER ROPE

"Take him, just take him!"

I had barely made it through the front door when my wife came barreling down the hallway, holding our three-month-old son, Peter, in front of her. Her arms were straight out and rigid, the baby dangling as far from my wife's body as possible. Peter was wearing nothing but a diaper, and from the way it sagged I was guessing it was fully loaded. His face was red and scrunched up, and his cries were so shrill and high-pitched I was surprised the glass in our windows didn't shatter.

"Wanda, what's wrong?" I said, taking Peter. I held him close, despite the foul smell coming from his diaper, and rocked him, making soft cooing noises in the back of my throat like a pigeon. The baby immediately quieted, looking up at me with a google-eyed expression of curiosity and wonder.

"Jason, he's been a nightmare all morning," Wanda said then started to cry herself, startling me. She'd never been much of a crier, not even when her parents died. "All he does is scream and scream and there's no making him stop!"

"Well, he seems fine now."

Wiping her eyes, Wanda stared down at the baby in my arms with what looked like contempt, but surely I was imagining it. "Of course he's well behaved for you. Always is. But when he's with me, all he does is cry and fuss. I swear, I haven't had a moment's peace since you left this morning."

"Well, I've got him for the next hour, you can just go sit down and relax."

I taught seventh grade English at a middle school only two blocks from our house, so it wasn't much trouble for me to come home on my lunch break. This was the first day of the new school year, and since Wanda had given birth over the summer, this was actually the first time she'd been alone with the baby for any extended period of time.

I took Peter into the living room and laid him on the changing table that was set up in the corner. Before becoming a father, the idea of changing dirty diapers disgusted me, but I found it wasn't nearly as gross as I'd feared. Maybe it was different when it was your own kid. As I sprinkled his bottom with baby powder before putting a fresh diaper on him, Peter giggled and squirmed around on the table like a happy worm.

Wanda had followed me into the room, and she stood a few feet away with her arms crossed, looking sullen. "It's not fair," she said.

"What's that?"

"I'm trapped in this house taking care of the baby while you get to go out in the world."

I sighed, lifting Peter and cradling him to my chest. "It's not like I'm out drinking with my buddies or playing golf. I'm working."

"Still, you don't know what it's like being here alone, having to do everything for the baby by yourself, no relief, no rest."

"Honey, it's only been about four hours."

"Seems a lot longer."

"Well, it's not all the time," I said, looking down at Peter. His eyes were closed, a thin line of drool leaking from the corner of his mouth, and I thought I could hear him snoring softly. "When I'm home, I'll pull my weight, you know that."

At first Wanda said nothing, but then she nodded and laughed shakily. "Sorry, I know I'm acting like a basket case. It's just been a really rough morning."

I smiled at her, trying for an expression that was sympathetic without being patronizing. "It's a huge adjustment, for both of us. All summer long you've had me around to help shoulder the burden, but now there's a part of the day where it's just you. I can only imagine how trying that must be. But keep in mind, it's only about a third of the day, and only the weekdays at that. You'll get the hang of it soon enough, then when I'm around you'll feel like I'm just in the way."

Wanda returned my smile, and I noticed the spots of color high up on her cheeks that indicated embarrassment. "I'm sure you're right. Just lost my head for a minute, that's all."

"Don't worry about it. What is it they say? Insanity is hereditary; you get it from your kids."

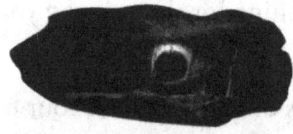

The next week and a half went well, or so I thought. I found out differently when I came home the following Friday afternoon.

I pulled into the driveway, and as soon as I stepped out of the car I could hear the baby crying inside. Not just crying, *screeching*. Sounded as if he were being scaled or skinned alive. Slamming the car door, I rushed to the house, bounding inside and homing in on the sound of the cries.

I found Wanda and Peter in the bedroom. The baby was lying in his crib, Wanda leaning over him with a bottle in one hand. Both mother and son were in tears, Wanda saying in a strident tone, "I know you're hungry, why won't you just take the damn bottle?"

"Wanda, what's going on here?"

She looked up at me with such a mixture of desperation and relief that it was almost frightening. "He won't stop. I don't know what's wrong with him. He doesn't need to be changed, he's not teething that I can tell, he doesn't have a fever, he hasn't been spitting up. All I can think is that he's hungry, but he won't take the bottle."

Frowning, worried that Peter might be really sick, I hurried to the crib. Taking the bottle from my wife, I inserted the nipple into the baby's mouth. Instantly the cries ceased, and Peter began sucking vigorously. He raised his little arms as if he were going to hold the bottle himself, and my frown melted into a smile.

"No, no, no," Wanda said, shaking her head, her already-tousled hair flying around her face as if caught in a high wind. "I've been trying to get him to take that bottle for an hour now and he was having none of it, but you waltz in and he takes it right away, no fuss no muss."

I glanced down at Peter, but he seemed unperturbed by his mother's outburst, intently focused as he was on sucking all the formula out of the bottle. "Honey, you need to calm down."

"I just think it's awfully interesting how he's always a perfect little angel for you, but with me he's like the spawn of Satan."

"Wanda, don't talk about Peter like that!"

"I'm sorry," she said, breaking down into fresh tears. She collapsed onto the bed, sobbing into one of the pillows. "I just feel like I'm losing my mind. It's nonstop, from the time you leave for work 'til you get home."

"I know you had some trouble that first day I went back to school, but I thought things had improved since then."

"No, they've gotten worse," she said, her voice muffled by the pillow.

Peter had turned his face away from the bottle, indicating he was done. I picked him up and laid him across my chest, his head on my shoulder, and bounced him while I patted his back. "Wanda, why didn't you tell me?"

"I didn't want you to think I was crazy."

"I'd never think that."

She sat up then, her eyes red and wet, her nose running. "I saw the way you looked at me last week, like you thought I was some histrionic nut job. Either that or the worst mother ever."

"I don't think anything of the sort."

"Well, it's how I feel," she said, taking a tissue from the box on the nightstand and sniffling into it. "I mean, I can't even take care of my own child. It's like he wants nothing to do with me."

Peter belched softly in my ear, and I put him back in the crib. He smiled up at the mobile that hung from the ceiling, reaching up as if to grab the little stars and moons that revolved above him. "You know that isn't true."

"Do I? Don't tell me you haven't noticed that even when you're here, he's only truly content when you're near him. If you so much as step out of the room, he starts crying and fussing and he'll take no comfort from me."

I gently poked Peter in the stomach with my finger a few times, making him smile and wriggle around, then I turned my full attention to Wanda. "Babies are unpredictable, you know that. One minute they can be perfectly happy then the next start bawling their eyes out for no discernible reason. It's not like it's personal."

Wanda got up and walked to me, peeking into the crib with what seemed to be trepidation. "It feels personal. Like he prefers you over me."

I put my arms around her and kissed her. "Don't be silly. Peter loves you, you're his mommy. It's impossible to know you and not love you, even for a three month old."

She buried her face in my chest, her hands clutching my back. "God, I feel like I'm cracking up. This isn't what I thought being a mother was going to be like at all."

"Tell you what, why don't you go lie down and I'll make us some dinner."

When Wanda looked up at me, I could see some of the old fire and sarcasm in her eyes that I'd first fallen in love with so many years ago. "You're going to make dinner? Are you trying to make me feel better…or worse?"

"Touché. I'll order delivery, how's that sound."

"Like a little bit of heaven."

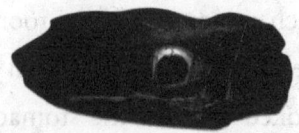

The next couple of months were really rough. Rarely did I come home from work that I didn't find both Wanda and Peter crying. And when I was home, she never wanted to be alone with the baby. If she changed him or fed him, she insisted I be within Peter's line of sight. She claimed it was the only way she could do anything with him without him pitching a fit.

And I had to admit, I did start to notice how the baby seemed to cry nonstop when I wasn't in the room with him. Anytime I left mother and son alone together—if I went to take a shower, to grade papers in the spare bedroom we used as my office, outside to do lawn work—the entire time I could hear the baby crying, and eventually Wanda's frustrated pleas for me to come back. It began to get tiring, and I started to look forward to going to work. Peter had both of us up several times every night—I was lucky to get four or five hours of sporadic sleep—but he did seem to go back down faster when I got up with him than when Wanda did.

But did I think this meant that the baby loved me more than he loved her? Not at all. Granted, I was just a middle school teacher and not a trained psychologist, but I figured the baby was picking up on all of Wanda's tension and aggravation and was merely responding to it. I truly believed that children could sense the emotions of their parents, and an unhappy parent could often result in an unhappy child. If only Wanda could relax around the baby, I just knew she'd find Peter to be much more compliant and joyful.

At one point we even took the baby to see his pediatrician, Dr. Stanfield, who assured us that Peter was fine and healthy. He also told us that it was normal for newborns to spend so much of the day fussing and that there were a myriad of reasons for this, none of which were bad parenting. Wanda nodded and thanked the doctor when we left, but I could see she was unconvinced.

On a Tuesday afternoon, while I was trying to get a bunch of 13 year olds interested in *A Separate Peace*, Mrs. Jenkins—Principal Moncrief's secretary—stuck her head in the door of my classroom and said, "Sorry to interrupt, but you have an emergency phone call from your wife."

The whole world seemed to lose focus at that moment, and my skin felt tight, as if my skeleton were growing and about to burst forth as if from a cocoon. All I could think was, *Something's happened to the baby, something's happened to Peter.* I left Mrs. Jenkins to watch the class and I rushed down to her office. The button for line 1 was flashing, but I hesitated to push it, afraid of what might be waiting on the other end of that line.

Finally, I swallowed my fear, picked up the phone, and punched the button. Even before I spoke, I could hear Peter crying in the background and I let out the breath I hadn't even been aware I was holding. No matter what it was, Peter wasn't dead. I had been trying to deny it, but that had been the root of my fear.

"Wanda?" I said, my voice quavering.

"Oh Jason, thank God. You've got to come home right away."

"Why, what's wrong? Is Peter sick, did he get hurt?"

"No, he just won't stop crying."

I felt my grip tighten on the receiver, and my voice was shaking for a different reason when I said, "You pulled me out of class because the baby is crying?"

"He won't quit! I've done everything, and he just won't quit!"

"Wanda, do you realize you scared me half to death? I was convinced that something terrible had happened."

"But Jason, can't you hear him?"

"Dr. Stanfield told you this was normal."

"Then why doesn't he act this way around you?" she shrieked so loudly I held the phone away from my ear. "It's only with me that he acts like this."

"If you'd just calm down and—"

"And don't try to feed me anymore of that psychobabble bullshit about how he's just reacting to my frustration. I'm telling you, he's doing this on purpose."

"Wanda, that's ridiculous."

"Easy for you to say. Now just get your ass home and get him to shut the fuck up so I can think straight again. I swear, his cries are drilling into my brain like a goddamn ice pick."

I was still angry, but I was growing increasingly concerned as well. Wanda had never been much of a cusser, but she was now dropping them like a character in a Quentin Tarantino movie. Something was obviously wrong—not with Peter, but with my wife—and I figured it would be best for me to see if Moncrief could find a sub for the rest of the afternoon so I could get home.

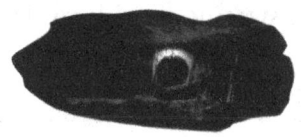

"Wanda, this has got to end."

I was sitting in the recliner, cradling Peter in my arms. I'd fed and changed him shortly after getting home, and now he was gurgling up at me while he played with the buttons of my shirt.

161

"Don't tell *me*," Wanda said, pacing back and forth in front of me, "talk to your son."

"I'd do that except he's only five months old and can't speak."

"Five months old or not, he knows exactly what he's doing."

"And what's that supposed to mean?"

Wanda glanced at Peter then lowered her voice, as if afraid he'd hear her. "He hates me."

I blinked at my wife, thinking at first that she must be joking, but her expression was dead serious. "You think the baby hates you?"

"Oh, I know he hates me. It's rather obvious, not like he tries to hide it or anything."

"Honey, do you have any idea how that sounds?"

"Sounds like the truth to me. I mean, just look at him. Before you got here he was raising almighty hell, but now that you're home he's all sweetness and light. How do you explain that?"

I didn't respond right away, looking up at my wife as if at a stranger. Since Peter had been born, she'd become another person, one I didn't recognize. She even looked different, large dark bags under her eyes, hair unkempt and often unwashed, some days not even getting out of her nightgown. She'd developed the habit of biting her nails, which she'd never done before, sometimes gnawing on them until her fingertips were ragged and bloody.

"Wanda," I said slowly, trying to keep my voice neutral and non-confrontational, "I think maybe you need to talk to someone."

She laughed, the sound hard and sharp. "What, you mean a shrink? I knew you thought I was crazy."

"I don't think you're crazy, but there's obviously something wrong here."

"You're right about that, and that something's name is Peter. He hates me, and he's trying to drive me insane."

I got up from the recliner and put the baby in his bassinet. He fussed a little but then quieted when he saw I wasn't leaving him. Couldn't say I blamed him—the way Wanda was acting right now, I wouldn't want to be left alone with her either.

"Look," I said, turning back to Wanda, "I'm not saying this is your fault. There's something that happens to some women after they give birth, something chemical. I've been reading up on postpartum depression, and there are treatments, medications, that can help."

"So you want to just drug me up to shut me up, is that it?"

"No, it's not like that. I just want to help."

"There's nothing you can do to help," she said, deflated. "I'm just going to have to learn to live with this, I guess. This is my life now."

She covered her face with her hands and started to cry, and the sound pierced my heart. No matter what she was going through, she was still my wife and I loved her. I didn't want to see her suffer. I went to her, put my arms around her, and whispered assurances in her ear.

When she had regained control of herself again, I said, "I think maybe we should hire someone."

"Hire someone?"

"You know, to help out with the baby."

"Like a nanny?"

"I'm not saying we'll get Fran Drescher in here or anything, but I think you need some help during the day while I'm at work."

At first Wanda looked like she was going to protest, but then she sagged against me and said, "Yes, please, I'd like that. But can we afford it?"

"I'll work it out."

Her name was Grace Cochram. There were no cliché fantasies of engaging in an illicit affair with this nanny. Grace was sixty-eight and looked even older. Still, she was energetic for her age and proved more than capable of keeping up with Peter.

The baby seemed to take to her almost immediately. A grandmotherly figure, Grace would often sing Peter little songs she made up herself, and he would smile, and clap his hands as if applauding her performance. In the beginning Wanda grumbled a bit about how her own child preferred a stranger over her, but soon enough she just seemed grateful to have someone to share the load.

Although, in all honesty Grace did more than simply share the load. Instead of Grace merely helping Wanda with the baby, it began to seem more that Wanda was helping Grace with the baby, a subtle distinction but one that put Grace more in the mothering role. I'd be lying if I didn't say it was a bit troubling, but there were no more instances of Wanda calling me at work and I always came home to a peaceful house. In fact, Wanda began to seem like her old self again, the woman I knew before Peter came, so rather than complain, I chose instead to just be thankful.

Grace wasn't a live-in or anything, worked Monday through Friday from 9 a.m. until 5 p.m., but within no time she seemed like a full-fledged member of the family. She often stayed after her shift ended and had dinner with us. On my birthday, which fell on a Saturday, she showed up to surprise me with a gift of cologne that I knew did not come cheap, especially not in the size she gave me. She even spent part of Christmas with us. With both Wanda's and my parents being deceased, Grace was a great source of advice and guidance for

165

two new parents trying to learn as they went.

After she had been with us for two months, Grace pulled me aside one evening shortly after I'd returned home from work. Wanda was in the bedroom napping, and Peter was in his bouncy chair in the living room, staring around as if it were a magical land that held nothing but mystery and beauty. Grace seemed a bit ill at ease, which surprised me. She normally seemed so comfortable around me.

"I hate to even bring this up," she said, wringing her liver-spotted hands. "I mean, it isn't really my place, I realize."

"Grace, you can say anything to me. Just spit it out."

"Well, sir, I know you pay me to look after the little one during the day, and I'm happy to do so. He's a real pleasure, an almost ideal child. But…"

"But what?" I prompted when she seemed hesitant to continue.

"It's your Mrs., sir."

"Wanda? What about her?"

"When it's just the two of us in the house with the baby, she doesn't want anything to do with Peter. She won't even hold him. If he starts to cry, she doesn't make a move to go comfort him. As I said, I realize it is my job to tend to the boy's needs, but it just seems strange to me that a mother would not react instinctively when her baby cries, that a mother would not want to hold her child in her arms as much as possible."

I didn't respond at first. This was what I had feared but not wanted to face directly. During the day, Grace took care of the baby, and after I returned home and on the weekends, I took care of the baby. I was always the one who got up with Peter in the night, which meant I dragged through work the next day. It was as if Wanda had removed herself entirely from our child's care, and that was more than just strange. It was disturbing.

"I appreciate your concern, Grace," I said, my voice a bit distant, staring off toward Peter.

"But I shouldn't be sticking my nose in where it doesn't belong. I do apologize."

"Oh no, not at all. I'm glad you came to me with this."

I noticed a blush creeping into her sallow cheeks. "It's just that these are important times for the bonding of mother and child. I'd hate to see her miss out on the experience."

"Thank you, Grace."

She nodded, kissed her fingertips then touched them to my cheek, and left.

I confronted Wanda about it later that night as we sat at the dinner table. She shoved her plate away, crossed her arms, and threw daggers at me with her eyes. "I don't see what the problem is."

"Honey, it's like you're isolating yourself from the baby."

She snorted a dry laugh. "Trust me, it's not like he

wants me around."

"Oh Wanda, I thought we were past this, I really did."

"The truth is, he's happier in someone else's care, and I'm happier not having to feel his hatred for me. Hiring Grace was the best thing we ever did."

I was more than a bit horrified by what I was hearing. Wanda spoke as if she'd washed her hands of the baby, given up her role as his mother. I also noticed how she never called Peter by his name. It all left me with an empty, hollowed-out feeling in my gut.

"I still think you should consider talking to someone. I just don't think this is healthy."

"What the fuck would you know about it?" she said, pushing away from the table. "You're not the one with a kid who can't stand to be around you."

She stormed out of the room, leaving me alone with my confusion and worry.

I was at a complete loss as to what to do, so I chose to do nothing. That may sound cowardly or weak, but I felt helpless to change the situation.

Things continued on pretty much as they were, Wanda

retreating from Peter while Grace and I shared the responsibility of caring for him, until about four months after Grace had started in our employ. I woke up from a nightmare in which Peter was sinking in quicksand, crying and holding his hands out toward Wanda, who simply stood there and watched dispassionately as our son was sucked under. I lay panting against the pillow, my eyes finding the glow of the digital clock. It was 3:24 a.m. Peter would probably be up for a feeding in the next half hour. I became aware of a soft sound nearby, but it took me a moment to realize it was my wife weeping into her pillow.

"Wanda," I said, placing a hand on her back. "What's wrong?"

At first it seemed she wasn't going to respond, but then she turned her face toward me. With no light but the moon filtering in through the windows, I could make out only the faintest impression of her profile, but I could feel her desperation and pain buffeting me like a wind. "That's what I'd like to know," she said. "What's wrong, what exactly is wrong with me? I'm some kind of monster."

"Honey, no."

"Yes, I am. I have nothing to do with my own son, let a stranger be more of a mother to him than I am. You're right, it isn't healthy. More than that, it's unforgivable."

"You're just having a rough time, this isn't uncommon among new mothers."

169

She sat up, leaning her back against the headboard. "It's been more than five months, and not only have I abandoned my child, I've actually grown to resent him. It's like I view him as some kind of enemy, out to get me. If that isn't madness I don't know what is."

I reached out into the darkness and took her hand, feeling her squeeze my fingers. While it broke my heart to see her suffering, I had to admit I was happy to hear her saying these things. Finally, Wanda seemed to be seeing reason, recognizing the irrationality of her recent behavior. "What do you want to do?" I asked, hoping she was finally willing to see a therapist.

"I want to let Grace go."

I was so stunned by this response that I think I actually recoiled as if slapped. "What? But Grace is wonderful with Peter."

"She really is. She's a lovely woman and has been a blessing, but she's doing the job that I should be doing. I've been using her as a crutch, as an excuse to withdraw more and more from my duties as a parent. I need to start taking care of Peter myself, and I'm afraid I'll never do that as long as Grace is around. Do you understand?"

"I do." And I did. It would pain me to have to relieve Grace of her duties, but I wanted to see my wife take her rightful place in our child's life, I wanted her get over her recent problems and become the mother I knew she could be.

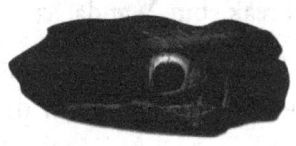

Grace took it better than I expected. In fact, she actually seemed delighted that Wanda had finally taken an interest in raising Peter. She promised to keep in touch, and we made plans to have dinner the following week. When she said her goodbyes to the baby, it was almost as if he could understand. Normally so calm in Grace's arms, Peter cried a little and clung to her when I tried to take him back, as if he did not want to be parted from his nanny.

I must admit that the house felt a bit empty without Grace, I'd grown so accustomed to her being around. It was actually sort of silly; after all, she did most of her work while I was at school, but I'd gotten used to seeing her tending to Peter when I arrived home every day. Still, I was looking forward to it just being the three of us again. Me, Wanda, and Peter. A family.

I was a bit nervous that first morning I left Wanda and the baby alone again. I could tell Wanda was nervous too but trying to put on a brave face, determined to prove that she could do this without any help. Peter was still sleeping when I left, but I hoped—for his sake and Wanda's—that things would go well while I was gone.

I worried the entire day. I was tempted to run home

during my lunch break, but Wanda had told me not to. It was like she was trying to make a point—to both of us. I respected her request and ate lunch in the teacher's lounge, but I kept my cell phone close by and barely resisted the urge to call and check on things. At the end of the day, I did not dawdle. I gathered my things and rushed to my car. In the warm months I often walked to work, living so close to the school, but during winter I drove the two blocks. I was home in minutes.

When I walked into the house, I immediately heard what I'd feared I'd hear…crying. I followed the sound to the bedroom and found Wanda pacing back and forth in front of the bed, bouncing the baby in her arms while he screamed and squirmed. His face was a disturbing shade of purple.

"I guess I don't have to ask how it went," I said.

Wanda glanced at me, her eyes glassy, almost like the eyes of a corpse. "More of the same. The entire four months Grace was here, he was so well behaved and happy. But today it has been nonstop crying."

I could have mentioned that after four months of Wanda avoiding the baby, he probably no longer recognized her, but I smartly held my tongue. I sat down my satchel full of papers to be graded and held out my arms. "Give him to me, let me see if I can calm him down."

"No!" she said vehemently, swinging the baby around, away from my grasping hands. "I'll do it."

172

"Really, I don't mind."

"Well, I do. He's just going to have to get used to me whether he likes it or not."

I watched Wanda resume pacing and bouncing the baby, but the way she jiggled him up and down it looked like she was trying to get the last penny out of a piggybank. "Honey, you're being too rough. You need to bounce him gently."

"What, you think I don't know how to take care of my own baby?"

"No, I'm just saying you might be scaring him bouncing him that hard."

"Fine, then you can have him," she said, practically thrusting Peter into my arms. "But he *will* get used to me. He doesn't have to love me, but he will learn to tolerate me. I'll be damned if I'll let him win."

With that, she left the room. I looked down at Peter, who had stopped crying but looked vaguely disoriented. No wonder, the way she was jerking him around, he probably felt as if he'd just come off a rollercoaster.

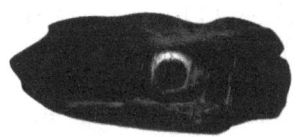

Over the next two weeks, Wanda developed a parenting style that seemed more mercenary than anything. Peter's feedings became force-feedings, his pacifier brandished at him like a weapon. When she spoke to the baby, it was in clipped, curt tones; when she rocked him, it was as if she were shaking an Etch-a-Sketch clean. Even when I was home, she insisted on being the one to care for Peter, which assured that he spent almost all his waking hours crying. I knew he was simply reacting to Wanda's aggressiveness.

I begged her to let me hire Grace back, but she refused. I had a private conversation with Grace in which she agreed with Wanda, believing that Peter simply needed to get used to being cared for by his mother. However, after I invited Grace over one evening and she witnessed the situation firsthand, even she told Wanda she'd be happy to start lending a hand again. Wanda's response was a chilly, "No thanks."

Finally, I had to put my foot down. Wanda seemed to be terrorizing the child, and I could not allow that to continue. Wanda still refused to see a therapist, insisting it was Peter who had the problem, not her. I really started to worry that there was something seriously wrong with my wife, a chemical imbalance triggered by childbirth maybe—I thought I'd read somewhere that that could happen. As much as it pained me to admit, I feared she may hurt Peter, even if unintentionally Or worse. When I was home, I never left her alone with him, and I insisted that we rehire Grace.

Wanda relented, but she wasn't happy about it. She turned cold toward me, didn't speak to me unless she had to, acting as if I'd betrayed her somehow. Grace reported that the warm, friendly woman Wanda had once been was no more. Wanda wouldn't let Grace do much other than warm bottles and occasionally change dirty diapers. For the most part, Wanda wanted to do it all, and Grace said that Peter cried almost nonstop.

Things went on like this for the next three weeks. I knew something had to be done, Wanda had to get help, even if it was involuntary. I was thinking of contacting some therapists and seeing what courses of action may be available to me.

But before I could, I got the phone call at work.

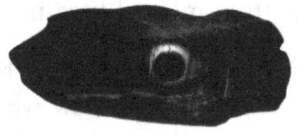

It wasn't Wanda who called me, but Grace.

"She fired me," she said.

"What?"

"Your Mrs. She told me my services were no longer required and told me to leave the premises."

"That's ridiculous. What happened?"

"She was acting very strange today. I mean, stranger than usual. She kept talking softly to the baby, almost whispering, and at first I couldn't really make out what she was saying. But then I got close enough and clearly heard her say,

'You think you're so clever, making everyone believe I'm crazy. Well, I wasn't before you started your little campaign of torture, but I certainly am now. You happy? You've driven me completely over the brink. You've left me no choice; I have to do it.'"

I felt cold, even though I was sweating. "Do what? What does she have to do?"

"I don't know," Grace said, sounding near tears, "but it scared me when I heard her talking like that, the tone of voice she used. I went up and took the baby and told her I thought she needed to lie down and rest. I planned to call you as soon as I was out of earshot, but instead she practically wrestled Peter away from me and fired me. Trust me, I didn't want to go, but she threatened to call the police and have me arrested for trespassing. I didn't know what else to do. So I came out to my car and called you on my cell. I'm sitting out front of the house now. What do you want me to do?"

"Wait right there, I'll be home in just a minute or two."

I hung up and told Mrs. Jenkins I had to go home, not even waiting to see if they were able to find a sub. On my way to the car, I used my cell to try to call the house, but the phone just rang until the answering machine picked up. I called Wanda's name several times, imploring her to pick up the phone, but there was no answer. That did not bode well, and I ran the two stop signs between the school and the house.

Grace's car was parked at the curb out front, and she got out of the car as soon as I pulled up. Without even stopping to say anything, I hurried to the front door, Grace behind me. I tried the door and it was unlocked; I stepped inside and was assaulted by silence.

The silence was damning. I was so used to Peter's incessant crying when he was alone with Wanda that the quiet of the house at this moment seemed a confirmation of my very worst fear. "Wanda?" I called out tentatively. "Where are you?"

And then I heard Peter, and my heart expanded like a balloon about to burst. But the baby wasn't crying—he was laughing. I followed that laughter like a trail of breadcrumbs, Grace moving along behind me quicker than I thought possible for someone her age.

The laughter was coming from our bedroom, a delighted trilling giggle. The door was shut, and I pushed it open, not sure what I expected to find.

At first I couldn't process what I was seeing, couldn't make my brain accept the reality of it. Only when I heard Grace scream behind me and sensed her turn away did the full force of what was before me truly hit.

The chair from Wanda's vanity, toppled on its side. The bed unmade, the sheet tied to the light fixture. Wanda dangling, her feet not touching the ground. Her face the color of a bruise, her tongue lolling out and looking somewhat

177

bloated. Peter sitting on the floor beneath her, laughing and clapping his hands as he looked up at his mother.

Finally freed from my paralysis, I ran to the dresser and rummaged through one of the drawers until I found the pocketknife my father gave me when I was 14. I righted the chair and quickly cut Wanda down, carrying her dead weight in my arms and laying her on the bed. I knew it was too late, but I checked her pulse anyway, confirming what I already knew.

Wanda was dead.

I could hear Grace in the hall, talking to a 911 operator on the phone. I grabbed Peter up, not wanting him to have to see his mother like this for a second more. As I hurried him from the room, he held his arms out toward the bed, giggled once more, and said his first word.

"Mama."

MEAT MARKET

The flashing lights dazzle my eyes, endlessly shifting in a kaleidoscopic pattern of color—icy blue, sizzling red, cool green. Out on the dance floor, men gyrate rhythmically in one mass orgy of flesh. It looks less like a group of individuals than one large body swaying to the blaring music. Four large speakers are set about the dance floor, one at each corner, and the music is so loud I can practically feel my eardrums thrumming in my head. The vibrations of the tidal wave of sound make my teeth rattle in my gums and my insides quiver like Jell-O. The air is close, and the place is filled with the musky odor of men. Sweat and semen and the yeasty aroma of alcohol, a blended smell that makes me think of ripe armpits and succulent balls.

The far wall is dominated by a group of television

monitors, all playing different programs: one shows an old episode of *Wonder Woman*, another *Absolutely Fabulous*, still another *Maude*. The bar runs the length of the opposite wall, a long mahogany bar polished with spit, booze, and vomit, most of the imitation-leather swivel barstools occupied by men—mostly older—who sit watching the young, hard bodies on the dance floor with the serious single-mindedness of tigers stalking their prey.

I stand just a few feet from the bar, leaning casually against the wall, a cigarette dangling from my full lips and my hands stuffed into the pockets of my tight black jeans. From beneath my darkly tinted glasses, my eyes watch the dance floor every bit as intently as the old men at the bar. The strobing lights illuminate them in snatches before plunging them back into darkness, teasing glimpses that feed my hunger. I let my gaze randomly alight on different men, sizing them up, then dismissing them for one reason or another—this one is too short, that one too fat, another too unkempt. I have a specific type from which I seldom deviate, and I know that if I am patient, I will eventually find someone who is just my taste.

And I am right.

In the middle of the dance floor, I catch sight of a young man who is dancing alone. The attitude he gives off like a scent is that he isn't so much dancing by himself as he is dancing with *everyone*. He is of average height, slight build, longish black hair with blonde roots flopping sloppily over one eye. He wears leather pants and a red velvet vest with nothing underneath. As he dances, his hands glide sensuously over his bare chest, his long skinny fingers teasing his pink nipples until they are hard. His eyes are closed and his face set in an expression of total concentration. This is a young man who takes his dancing very seriously. I watch him for some minutes through the opening/closing curtain of convulsing bodies on the dance floor, my eyes skirting over his milky white skin and fashionably emaciated body. The strobe lights paint his skin in the alternating colors of the rainbow, as if his flesh is a canvas to be painted on. I feel my desire rise like a bloated corpse from a watery grave. I have to have him—it is as simple as that.

I part my lips slightly and let my smoldering cigarette stub drop to the floor, where I grind it mercilessly with the thick heel of my scuffed boot. I remove my glasses and place them into the breast pocket of my brown leather jacket; my eyes are my best feature, a faint shade of blue that seems to draw other colors in and reflect them back like a prism. I run a hand casually through my thick mane of wavy, honey-colored hair, and undo the top two buttons of my black button-down shirt, revealing just a shock of wiry chest hair. Plastering on my most charming and alluring smile, I start making my way through the sweaty throng on the dance floor, honing in on my lone dancer.

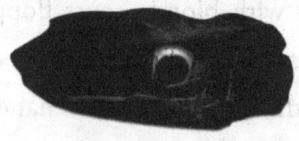

The music pounded in Philip's ears like an atomic explosion, raising goosebumps on his skin. Heedless of the other hundred dancers, he moved to his own unique sense of rhythm and time, letting the music pour over him like an auditory waterfall. The multicolored strobe lights painted his body a garish mosaic as his hands roamed ceaselessly over his upper torso, always coming back to the sensitive nubs of his pale nipples. His feet stuck slightly to the sticky floor, so that each time he raised a foot, it peeled away. This resistance made him dance all the harder.

Out of the corner of his eye, Philip noticed a man striding purposefully across the dance floor, heading straight toward Philip. He smiled to himself, well accustomed to this type of bold advance. He never went to a club without being hit on, flirted with, or otherwise propositioned. Sometimes he was receptive, other times not, depending on his mood. And as Philip got a look at his potential suitor's well-defined muscles and the dazzling rainbows of his eyes, Philip decided he was in the proper mood tonight.

Without a word or any other form of communication, Philip turned to the man who had approached him, wrapped his arms around his neck, and started brazenly grinding against him. The man, dressed in extremely tight black clothing, responded with enthusiasm, his hands straying to Philip's buttocks. Philip stared into his dance partner's beautiful, rugged face, mesmerized by the way the lights danced in his crystalline eyes. Philip's hands moved down to the man's rock-hard chest, massaging the impressive pectorals, feeling the small, hard stones of the man's nipples through the thin material of his shirt. Philip became instantly hard, and he rubbed his erection against the man's thigh, the delicious friction sending an ecstatic, electrical thrill up Philip's spine.

The man, easily a foot taller than Philip, bent over and kissed the side of Philip's neck, just below the ear. Philip threw his head back and placed a hand on the back of his dance partner's head. The man continued to nibble at Philip's throat, delivering pleasurable love-bites that would look like bruises in the morning. It was as if everyone else on the dance floor had disappeared, and Philip and this sensual stranger were the only two people left in the club.

Philip moved his lips close to his dance partner's ear, still having to shout in order to be heard over the relentless dance music. All thumping bass and trilling synth notes, the baby-voiced singer crooning words that couldn't be deciphered at this volume. Philip didn't recognize the song, and yet he felt every beat in his soul. An external heartbeat to match his own. "Do you want to go somewhere a little more private?"

The man suddenly covered Philip's lips with his own,

shoving his tongue forcefully into Philip's eager mouth. The man's fingers trailed lightly and teasingly up Philip's stomach and chest, finally pinching Philip's nipples in a pleasurably painful vise. Breaking the kiss, the man grabbed Philip's hand and started leading him off the dance floor, all without speaking a word.

Philip expected to be led to a restroom, or perhaps the pool room in the back, but instead they exited the club and headed for the loose-gravel parking lot. After the cacophony of the dance floor, the comparative quiet of the night was almost overwhelming; it was like going deaf. The night breeze was warm and balmy, the stars twinkling down like happy fairies from Heaven.

"Where're we going?" Philip asked, walking close to the man's side.

"I have a van," the man answered, his voice deep yet melodic.

"Don't you want to know my name?" Philip said playfully, leaning his head on the man's shoulder.

The man didn't reply for a moment, but then smiled down at Philip, his eyes catching the star-shine and beaming it back like headlights. "Sure," he said. "What's your name?"

"Philip. How about yours?"

"Dante."

"As in the guy who went to Hell and back?"

"The very same."

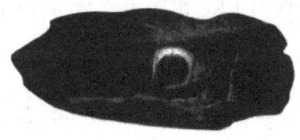

When we reach my van, painted as black as a witch's heart with darkly tinted windows, I shove the young man—Philip, he said his name was—up against the side of it and begin kissing him furiously. I can feel his hardness against my leg, and his need seems almost as desperate and all-consuming as my own. I fondle him through his pants, causing him to cry out and clutch my shoulders. In his urgency, he rips open my shirt—buttons flying like pearl bullets through the air—and begins kissing my chest, sucking hungrily at my nipples. I glance around and see other similar tableaus; couples groping one another right out in the open, cars rocking gently, windows fogged over by hot, urgent breath, ghostly shapes glimpsed through the steam. We are attracting no undue attention, just another pair of fornicating worshippers in a paradise of flesh.

Overcome by the heat of the moment, Philip starts to drop to his knees in front of me. "Whoa, now," I chide, taking him by the shoulders and pulling him back to his feet.

"I can't wait," Philip pants, running his spidery fingers through the golden hairs that cover my chest like a rug. "I *need* it."

"And you'll get it," I say, unhooking my keys from where they hang on my belt loop. I unlock the side door of the van, and it slides open like a huge, yawning mouth, ready to gobble us up like a vicious monster from some dark fairytale. Stepping aside like a proper gentleman, I usher Philip inside my van, just as I have done with so many young men like him in the past.

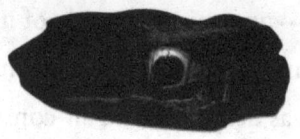

The air inside the van was somewhat musty and stale, but not unpleasantly so. The parking lot was poorly lit, and the tinted windows kept out what meager light there was, rendering the darkness of the van impenetrable. But after a few seconds, Philip's eyes began adjusting to the murkiness and he was able to make out exactly what he'd been expecting to find—a mattress. Predictable, but acceptable.

Dante climbed in behind Philip, pulling the door closed as he entered. Immediately, they were on one another, dropping to the mattress with Philip on bottom, wrestling around and tugging at each other's clothes, making keening, animalistic noises deep in their throats.

Philip gasped as he felt Dante's teeth at his throat, sharp and insistent. "Like to bite, do you?" he said into Dante's ear.

"Oh yeah," Dante answered, his voice heavy with passion. "I like to give it rough, boy."

"So do I," Philip said, baring his own teeth—teeth that were much too long and pointy to belong in a human mouth—and sinking them deep into Dante's flesh, at the juncture where his neck met his shoulder. Dante cried out, his body going rigid with pain and shock. Philip held him tightly, rolling over so that he was now on top, all the while keeping his mouth firmly attached to Dante's throat, drinking deep from the Fountain of Life and Eternal Youth.

When the deed was done, Philip sat back and wiped his mouth with the back of his hand. Dante's lovely eyes, now glassy and empty, stared blankly up at the roof of the van. Philip reached out and shut Dante's lids. A pair of tinted glasses poked out of a pocket in Dante's jacket. Philip snatched these up and placed them on his own face. Call him sentimental, but he liked to keep some kind of memento from these little trysts of his.

Sliding the door open, Philip stepped out into the parking lot. Several people were nearby, but none of them were paying him the least bit of attention; they were engrossed in liaisons of their own. He closed the door and locked it with Dante's keys—the keys he would deposit in a trashcan when he went back inside the club. After all, the night was young and there was more dancing to be done before dawn.

NATURAL SELECTION

The house was barely standing. Sometime in the past a fire had obviously broken out in the back end, and the roof there had collapsed. The front door was long gone, only a rectangular coffin-shape of blackness inviting them into a grave.

Lowell started toward the opening, but Dru stilled him with a hand. "Structure seems unstable. Are you sure it's safe?"

Lowell smiled. "Is anything in this godforsaken world truly safe?"

Having no response to that, she released him to enter the house and she followed after one last look around the street to scan for scavengers or thieves. She saw and heard no one; they appeared to be alone in this deserted neighborhood.

Inside, she found Lowell moving slowly, testing each

floorboard before putting his full weight down. Lowell was no fool, and she had taught him caution was a necessary survival skill in this decimated world. The place showed signs of semi-recent habitation from squatters, threadbare blankets and food packaging and an old metal trashcan where a fire had obviously been built right in the middle of the room. Such a homemade heating system had probably been responsible for the destruction at the back of the house.

As Lowell made his way slowly across the room, he talked. Things she'd already heard, but she recognized this was more for his benefit than hers so she allowed it: "Rick and I lived here when the sickness started to really spread. We knew it was serious but figured eventually doctors and scientists would get it under control, like they did the first time. Then more and more people started dying, world governments started to collapse, and we realized society itself was falling apart.

We stayed here as long as we could. This was our home, after all, and we had scrimped and saved for years in order to afford the down payment. We were stubborn and didn't want to leave. Eventually, food became scarce and nicer neighborhoods like this one used to be were being looted. So we packed up some stuff, only the necessities, and headed for the city where we hoped to find safety. What a joke. All we found there were those two creeps who killed Rick and would have killed me if you hadn't come along and stopped them."

Dru remained silent as Lowell reached a door in the far wall and opened it to reveal a small closet. He bent and pulled out a moldy cardboard box. "It's still here," he said with an almost child-like excitement. He pulled back the flaps and began rummaging through the contents. Dru stepped closer, thinking the box could contain nothing of importance since none of the people who had used this place as a temporary stopover had taken away with it.

Of course, she recognized that something's importance was often subjective and personal.

Lowell squatted on the floor and pulled out a dusty leather-bound photo album. Opening it, the first picture was of two beautiful young men in tuxedos, smiling at the camera from a world that no longer existed. One was only vaguely recognizable as Lowell himself.

"That's him," Lowell said, tears cutting tracks through the grime on his cheeks. "I had forgotten what he looked like, I could no longer picture the contours of the face I used to know as well as my own, but this is him. This is my Rick. Thank you for coming with me. I had to get his face back."

Silently, Dru stepped back outside, leaving her friend alone with his tears and memories.

HAUNTING AT STUMP LAKE

Justin Holley stood at the bottom of the gentle slope just shy of the waterline, staring out across the still dark waters of Stump Lake. The nearly full moon reflected three ghostly images of itself, one in each of the lake's bowls. Behind him, Justin could hear Adam and Wayne unloading the equipment. He heard no other sound, save for the cry of a lone loon somewhere in the game preserve to the left of the property. Certainly no ghostly crying.

Justin turned and made his way back up the slope to where he'd parked the Jeep, the small camper tethered behind. Adam and Wayne had laid out the equipment on a blanket and were checking it over.

Wayne glanced up at Justin and said, "So you really think this place is haunted?"

Justin shrugged. "I've never experienced anything my-self, but Ali swears that the last time we came out here, she heard someone crying down at the lake and saw an indistinct shape hovering over the water before dissipating."

Adam gave him a sideways glance. "Sure she didn't just hear a loon and see some mist?"

"I know, I know, and if it were anyone else, I'd think the same thing. But you guys know Ali, she's a believer but never goes around making claims of sightings. If she feels like she had an experience then I believe her. Regardless, she says she doesn't want to come back to the lake until we investigate. And since we plan to eventually build a house here, my wife refusing to set foot on the property could be problematic."

Wayne laughed. "Well, some husbands would pick a ghost over their own wives, but in your case, I think you're making the right call."

Justin bent and picked up one of the SB-7 spirit box-es, then glanced up to see Adam scanning the lake with the digital camera. They always started filming immediately upon reaching a location because ghosts didn't patiently wait to manifest until an investigation had officially begun.

"Did you guys hear anything more from Kayla?" Justin asked.

"Oh yeah," Wayne said. "She sent me a message on the way over here. Said she couldn't find any reports of con-firmed deaths here at the lake, but she did dig up one tidbit that might be relevant to us. Back in the '40s, a little girl went missing when her family was camping in the area. Wandered off and was never seen again. Authorities searched the woods for days, even had some divers come in to scour the lake. No sign of her. So I'd say, if they never found her—unless she was snatched by some crazy backwoods hillbilly child-napper—chances are she died somewhere around here, even if no body was ever found."

Justin nodded. "Sounds like a good place to start. Did she happen to find out the girl's name?"

Wayne pulled out his cell and scrolled through the texts. "Bethany Johnson."

"Okay," Justin said. "Let's start out by doing an EVP session down by the water."

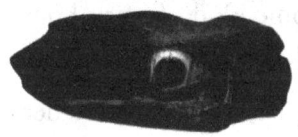

The Minnesota Paranormal Study Group had been founded in 2005, and Justin had done so many investigations with the group that he would be hard pressed to give an actual number if asked. There had been many memorable cases: Palmer House in Sauk Center, William A. Irvin ship in the Duluth harbor, The Old Train Depot in Duluth, and the Greyhound Bus Museum in Hibbing. He'd seen three full-bodied apparitions with his own eyes, and gotten photographic evidence from two locations—the St. Augustine Lighthouse and a sugar plantation, both in Florida. He'd had objects thrown at him, heard disembodied voices, and he'd never felt the worry that he felt right now.

It wasn't fear, but this case was different from all the others in that it was personal. Something here had frightened his wife and made the place that was meant to be their home someday, their sanctuary and refuge, into a place where she didn't feel comfortable. If Justin could fix that, then he needed to. They'd invested so much in this little lakeside haven. Not just money, but dreams. So many dreams. He had to take away whatever taint Ali's experience had put on the place so they could resume their dreaming.

At least he hoped he could. Ali often worried that Justin might bring some kind of spirit home with him from an investigation, so the notion that something was already waiting for them at the lake had unnerved her more than he'd ever seen, and more than he'd wanted to admit to the other members of the group. Even Justin's step-son had been affected. Normally the toughest of skeptics, his mother's apprehension seemed to have infected him as well.

So Justin had agreed to set up this overnight investigation to ease Ali's mind. If he found nothing, he knew she'd be placated though never a hundred percent at ease here, so he actually hoped to find some evidence of a benign spirit or one that simply needed assistance moving on.

If he found anything with a more sinister purpose for lingering here…well, he'd cross that bridge if he came to it.

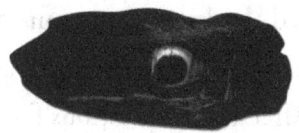

The three men gathered by the lake. Adam still had the camera, and Justin held the spirit box in one hand and an EMF reader in the other—to detect any fluctuations in the electromagnetic field. Wayne had the recorder for the Electronic Voice Phenomenon (EVP) session.

Most people were familiar with the concept, catching disembodied voices that couldn't be heard by the human ear, yet most people associated scratchy, staticky noise that could be interpreted a million ways. However, Justin had captured some EVPs in his time that were so clear as to be undeniable.

He nodded to Wayne to start recording, then Justin turned to gaze out across the water again and said loudly, "Is there anyone here with us tonight? Bethany Johnson, are you here? Did you die at the lake? Is there a reason you're lingering here?"

Justin paused between each question, giving the spirit time to answer. When he'd first started doing investigations, these sessions had made him feel pretty silly, but now it was old hat to him. Plus, he knew that some spirits wanted nothing more than a chance to be heard, to be acknowledged, so what might seem silly to others was actually a public service to those who were forgotten.

As he talked, he kept an eye on the EMF reader. A few fluctuations here and there, but nothing that suggested an unseen presence. After asking questions for a full five minutes, Justin stopped and nodded once again to Wayne who turned off the recorder.

"Should I go ahead and play it back?" Wayne asked.

Under normal circumstances, reviewing of the evidence would all take place after the investigation was completed, but Justin reminded himself that these weren't normal circumstances. "I guess. Let's see if we caught anything."

The three settled on the ground, Adam keeping the camera running and periodically scanning across the water. Wayne played back the EVP session, and they all leaned forward to listen. When they were able to run the audio through the computer and listen with headphones, they might pick up some sounds they missed now, but as it was they heard nothing. Justin asking questions, and only silence in answer. Wayne replayed it two more times, but the result remained the same. Nothing.

"Alicia's great and all," Adam said, "but don't you think it's at least possible that she just spooked herself?"

Justin thought about it for a moment then shook

his head. "No. Ali is unnerved by this kind of stuff, but she doesn't spook easily."

He knew his wife, he believed what she told him, but truth was he needed to give anyone who said they had a personal experience the benefit of the doubt. As someone who had been investigating the paranormal for over a decade, he knew how skeptical people could be and how that skepticism could turn into hurtful condescension. If pressed, he was sure he could get Adam and Wayne to admit they'd had personal experiences before that weren't caught on audio or video. Just because there was no tangible evidence, didn't always mean nothing was there.

"Okay, so what next?" Wayne asked.

Justin held up his left hand. "Spirit box."

Adam groaned. "Oh man, I hate that thing. I'm convinced that sound can induce seizures in some people like the voice of that old chick from *Entertainment Tonight* did back in the day."

The spirit box was a relatively new instrument in the team's arsenal. It worked by rapidly scanning radio frequencies, providing a discordant mix of white noise and audio fragments. The idea being that a spirit could manipulate the frequencies to send a message. The scanning was so fast that a single word here or there would not indicate anything, but if you got a string of words that formed coherent sentences, that would suggest a spirit was trying to communicate. The noise could be irritating—nails-on-a-chalkboard irritating—so Adam had a point.

Justin started the machine, and the stillness of the night was broken by the static-infused frenetic scanning. Every so often, a snippet of music or an errant word could be heard among all the auditory chaos, but nothing significant.

After five minutes of enduring the racket, Wayne said, "Is that enough? Can we move on?"

Justin nodded his agreement and was about to turn the machine off when two words came through clearly, one right after the other.

"*See...*"

"*Me...*"

"Whoa," Justin said. "Did you guys hear that?"

Adam and Wayne exchanged a glance before looking back to Justin, then down at the spirit box in his hand.

"Just two words," Adam said. "Could be coincidence they seemed to actually go together to form a sentence."

Justin had to admit Adam had a point. Number one rule of paranormal investigation was that you had to go in with a skeptical mind, otherwise you thought every cool draft and creaking floorboard provided irrefutable proof of life after death. That only served to give the field the reputation it had as being full of charlatans and shysters. No, you had to go in trying to debunk every bit of evidence, so that all that stood up in the end was the evidence that could not be debunked.

Still, one had to follow his instincts as well, and Justin's instincts told us those two words were more than mere coincidence.

"Bethany, was that you?" he asked the night.

At first there was nothing, but then the temperature dropped noticeably, causing Justin to shiver. Wayne apparently felt it as well, because he held out the digital thermometer. "Temperature just dropped seven degrees," he said.

Adam opened his mouth to say something, possibly another reminder that this too could be coincidence, but then the spirit box delivered another message. Not two words this time, but five.

"*Need...*"

"*You...*"

"*To...*"

"*See...*"

"*Me...*"

"Okay," Adam said. "That's a little more compelling."

"Who are you?" Justin called out. "Who is it that needs to be seen? Can you tell me your name?"

Another half a minute of static and then three more consecutive words, three words that when combined created a single name.

"*Bet...*"

"*And...*"

"*Knee...*"

Justin noticed the excitement in Adam and Wayne's eyes, but even more, he noticed the vapor puffing from their lips with each breath as the temperature continued to drop. Wayne checked the thermometer again. "Down ten more degrees," he said through chattering teeth. "I've never experienced a temp drop this far this fast."

Adam started pointing out toward the water. "Look! You guys seeing what I'm seeing?"

Justin turned his attention to the water line and saw the mist forming. Mist on the lake wasn't unusual, though this wasn't a blanket spreading slowly across the surface. It was an isolated clump right off the land, a ball of diaphanous smoke that twisted and morphed until it almost seemed to take on the shape of a crude face.

He knelt down at the edge of the water, heedless of the mud caking his pants and reached out toward the mist.

"Be careful," Adam said, tension causing his voice to sound slightly higher pitched than normal.

"I just want to see if I can feel anything, if the mist has any substance. Be sure to keep the camera on me."

The spirit box continued scanning frequencies in his hand, and a final message came through.

"*See...*"

"*What...*"

"*Happened...*"

At that moment, a small white hand shot up from the

water and latched onto Justin's wrist. The fingers were delicate and almost skeletal…but incredibly strong. Justin felt himself being jerked forward, and before he could even cry out, he splashed down into the water. At its deepest, the lake went down about twenty-five feet, but here at the shoreline it should have been much more shallow. And yet Justin seemed to sink and sink and sink as if he were out in the middle of an ocean.

He began to thrash and try to make his way back to the surface, but it was as if his body had turned to lead and he only continued his descent. His lungs burned as he held his breath, and panic began to gnash at his brain like rabid rats. One of Justin's greatest fears was deep water, and it was as if he'd been submerged in one of his worst nightmares.

The surface drifted farther and farther away until it seemed like an impossible dream, as distant and unreachable to him as the moon. When he could hold his breath no longer, he opened his mouth, expecting an onrush of brackish lake water to invade his windpipe, but instead he felt air fill his lungs. Surrounded by water, yet still he could breathe, as if he were encased in some type of bubble.

A lilting voice reached his ears, not making words but just humming a familiar tune. It took him a few seconds to place it as "Camp Town Races". It came to him, first faintly, but then gaining volume and clarity, and he turned his head to see the girl floating toward him. She was young, surely no older than ten, blond hair snaking around her head like Medusa's locks. Dressed in a bright yellow sundress, she inched closer to him until they were practically nose to nose.

Justin knew he should be frightened, but something about her radiated a calm that had a sedating effect on him. He didn't even flinch when she reached out and placed her hands to the sides of his head, her thumbs pressing against his eyes.

He felt an electric jolt, and a flash of brilliant light temporarily blinded him, and then...

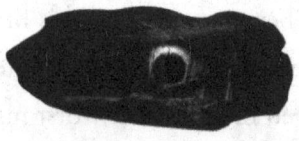

It unfolded before him like a home video playing just behind his eyes. The picture slightly grainy, the sound somewhat tinny. A young girl, her blond hair done up in high pigtails, her yellow dress so bright it was almost a supernova. Though he watched her from the outside, Justin experienced her feelings, experienced her thoughts.

She skipped toward the lake, humming "Camp Town Races" underneath her breath. Behind her, her parents were vague indistinct shapes. Her mother's voice rose sharply. While the words themselves were indecipherable, the critical tone was clear. As usual, she was picking at Bethany's father.

Nothing he did ever seemed to meet her standards, and she definitely let him know it.

Bethany felt sorry for her father, because she too seemed incapable of pleasing her mother. And yet she also felt sorry for her mother, because with the innocent wisdom of a child, Bethany understood that her mother found fault with everyone around her because secretly she found fault with herself.

In any case, Bethany did not want to think about these things, not on a beautiful day like today. The air was warm but not overly hot, the sky a pure crystalline blue with only a few clouds like gobs of whipped cream floating by. The water sparkled in the sunlight, looking almost like an undulating field of diamonds.

A fleeting shadow caused her to glance up, shielding her eyes with a hand, and she saw a large eagle soaring out above the water. It moved away from her, and Bethany found herself trailing after it, picking up speed to try to keep the regal bird in her sight. She wasn't supposed to wander beyond earshot of her parents, but she forgot that rule in her excitement. Besides, they weren't paying any attention to her.

Ahead of her, the eagle dipped lower toward the water and veered closer to the shoreline. Bethany went from a trot to an all-out run, her twittering laughter rising into the air like the carbonation bubbles of a soda. It was liking playing tag with the kids on the playground at school. She imagined she could catch up with the eagle and jump on its back as if it were a horse, and she'd fly it up to one of the clouds and take a nap there.

Caught up in the middle of this fantasy, Bethany became oblivious to the path before her. The lake's shoreline wasn't beachy but tangled with weeds, and her right foot caught in a particularly heavy clump and sent her toppling. Her arms pin-wheeled as she tried to keep her balance. Gravity won the battle, and she went down like a felled tree. Her head struck a half-buried stone, pain detonating inside her skull like an atomic explosion. Her vision grayed around the edges and she rolled over, splashing into the water.

The water!

Her parents had told her to stay out of the water, not to get her dress wet, and now she was submerged in it. She tried to sit up, to pull herself back onto dry land, but she became dizzy, and the graying edges began to eat up more of her vision like a spreading rash. She sputtered and gagged and realized her head had fallen beneath the surface of the water. She struggled to stand but the pain increased until her head felt as big as one of those massive balloons in the Macy's Thanksgiving Day Parade, only not as light. Her head felt heavy as a boulder, and it weighed her down. She felt herself floating, sinking, and as she breathed in another lungful of lake water, she lost consciousness.

Her last thoughts were of soaring high into the heavens on the back of the eagle...

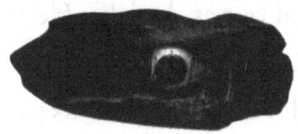

Another blinding flash of light and Justin's head broke the surface. He sucked in oxygen, sputtering and coughing. He realized he was kneeling in the shallow water, which came up only to his waist. Behind him, he heard Adam and Wayne laughing.

"Getting a bit clumsy in your old age, huh?" Wayne said.

Justin whirled around, getting shakily to his feet.

Adam pointed to his left hand. "I think that's pretty much ruined."

Justin glanced absently at the spirit box he still clutched in a vise-like grip then tossed it down into the water as he made his way to the shoreline. "Didn't you guys see it? Her hand grabbed me and pulled me right into the water."

Adam and Wayne exchanged a puzzled look. "We didn't see any hand," Wayne said. "Just looked like you lost your balance and toppled into the water."

"And you guys didn't think about coming in after me?"

Adam frowned at him, his expression one you might give to someone who said they saw little green men or pink elephants. "Come in after you? You fell in and got right back up. You were under for maybe half a second."

Justin stared out at the lake. He thought he detected just the slightest hint of a mist but it quickly dissipated. "Half a second? But it felt like…it seemed like…"

Wayne clamped a hand on his shoulder and said, "Tell us what happened from your perspective. What did you experience?"

After a few deep breaths to calm himself, Justin said, "She showed me. She showed me what happened to her the day she went missing."

"And?" Adam asked, aiming the camera at him.

"She wandered off, much farther than anyone realized. Then she fell, hit her head, tumbled into the water and lost consciousness. From there she got caught in the undercurrent which carried her even farther away. Somewhere out there, her bones are still down in the lake."

"So what do we do?" Wayne asked. "Do we need to find her remains and bury them? Figure out if she has any living relatives and contact them?"

Justin shook his head. "No, I don't think this is about a proper burial or bringing closure to her family. I think it's exactly what she told us—she needed me to see. She just wanted a witness, for someone to know what happened. I think she can rest now."

Adam looked uncertain. "Are you sure?"

"Honestly, no, but I think I'm right."

"So what do we do now?" Wayne asked. "Pack it in for the night?"

"Yeah. Why don't you guys get some burgers going on the grill while I dry out. Might as well crack out some beers while you're at it."

Adam and Wayne started toward the camper but then Wayne glanced back. "You coming?"

"In a minute," Justin said.

As his two friends and teammates wandered off, talking quietly among themselves, Justin stood at the edge of the lake, taking in the tranquil quality of the water, and let a small smile curl the corners of his mouth.

"Good night, Bethany. Sleep well."

UNKNOWN NUMBER

Summer 2003

Ethan sat outside at his favorite bistro, waiting for Roger to arrive for lunch, when his cell phone began to vibrate on the tabletop, indicating that he had a new text message. Assuming it would be Roger with some lame excuse for why he was late, Ethan flipped open his phone. But the text wasn't from Roger's number; the Caller ID identified it as an UN-KNOWN NUMBER. With a slight frown, Ethan opened the text.

HELLO. HOW R U?

Wondering who the message was from—none of his friends had blocked numbers that would come up as UN-KNOWN NUMBER—Ethan quickly texted back. DOIN FINE, WHO IS THIS?

The answer was almost immediate, as if the texter had been anticipating the question. SOMEONE CLOSE 2 U.

Ethan's frown deepened as his thumbs hovered over the keypad. His mind sifted through a mental Rolodex, looking for likely suspects. Could be Pam or Greg, or even his sister Julie. All three were pranksters by nature, and anyone could be the culprit. The question was, did he feel like playing along this afternoon?

Deciding the answer was no, he snapped the phone closed and set it back on the table. He was too preoccupied to participate in some silly game, his thoughts focused on Roger and the conversation that would ensue when he finally arrived. It had been a week since he'd asked Roger to move in with him, and Roger had said he needed time to think it over. Just this morning he'd received the call; Roger had made a decision but wanted to tell him in person. Ethan wasn't sure if that was a good sign or bad.

The fact that Roger was almost a half hour late for their lunch date certainly didn't bode well. If it was good news, surely he'd be in a rush to get here and share it. If it was bad news, might Roger want to dawdle, procrastinate, put off breaking his heart?

The phone began vibrating again. Annoyed, but still hoping it might be a message from Roger, he snatched it up and read the new text.

WHY R U IGNORING ME?

The UNKNOWN NUMBER again.

With a grunt of frustration, he responded. NOT IN THE MOOD FOR GAMES. TELL ME WHO THIS IS OR LEAVE ME ALONE.

While he waited, he sipped at his now-lukewarm latte. The sound of a car backfiring somewhere close by caused him to start, and he spilled his drink down the front of his shirt. "Damn it," he grumbled, grabbing his napkin and blotting at the stain. On the table, the phone vibrated again, actually moving across the surface as if anxious to have its message read.

B MORE CAREFUL WITH THAT DRINK, UR MAKING A MESS OF URSELF.

Ethan started again, this time knocking his cup completely off the table, spilling his latte all over his shoes. He stood quickly, sending the metal chair clattering to the ground, looking all around—across the street, at the cars that drove by, at the other customers sitting outside, at the pedestrians that passed, at the windows of the nearby buildings. Whoever was sending him these texts could obviously see him, was watching him from somewhere close.

SOMEONE CLOSE 2 U, the mystery texter had said. Whoever it was hadn't been lying.

"Everything all right, sir?" a waiter who'd been cleaning off one of the other outside tables asked him.

"Yes, just fine," Ethan said, righting the chair and taking his seat again. "There was a bee, got a little too close, I'm terribly allergic. Could I get another latte?"

"Certainly," the waiter said, retrieving Ethan's now-empty cup from the ground, depositing it in the trash, and hurrying back inside.

Ethan stared down at the phone still clutched in his hand. He was overreacting. Sure, it unsettled him to know he was being watched, but this was still more than likely just a prank. In fact, if he had to guess he'd say this whole *When a Stranger Calls* setup had Greg's fingerprints all over it.

He took a deep breath and texted back. VOYEUR-ISM, HUH? KIND OF PERVY.

The response came quickly. I'VE BEEN WATCH-ING U 4 A WHILE.

Ethan chuckled; this definitely felt more and more like Greg. HOPE YOU ENJOYED THE SHOW.

He'd barely hit send when he got a reply. I HAVE, BUT WHY DIDN'T U WEAR THE BLUE SHIRT?

Ethan was just about to text back, *BECAUSE IT WAS TOO HEAVY ON A WARM DAY*, when his fingers suddenly froze. The hairs on the nape of his neck stood up. How did the mystery texter know that this morning Ethan had originally put on his deep blue button-up before settling on the peach tee he now wore? He had actually stepped outside his apartment building in the blue shirt before deciding he would be too stuffy in it. He'd gone back inside to change. Had Greg been watching him since early morning?

Impossible. Shortly after changing and leaving the house, Ethan had received a call from Greg that came up on the Caller ID as Greg's home number, which originated far across town.

So maybe it wasn't Greg, and Julie was in college out of state. Pam? Possible, but why would she go to the lengths of following him around all day? None of it made sense.

His thoughts were interrupted when the waiter brought him a second latte. Ethan smiled distractedly at him and paid for the drink. Before he had time to take a sip, a new message arrived.

WAITER'S CUTE, HOPE U GAVE HIM A BIG TIP.

"I get it," Ethan said aloud, causing some of the other patrons to glance his way. "You can see me. Well, can you see this?" Ethan stuck up the middle finger of his right hand and waved it around in the direction of the street. A table of elderly women gave him dirty looks then turned back to their salads.

A new text came in almost immediately. THAT'S NOT VERY NICE OF U.

At his wit's end, Ethan responded, punching the small keys with so much force it was a wonder he didn't crack his phone's casing.

I'VE HAD JUST ABOUT ENUFF OF YOUR

BULLSHIT. WATCH ME ALL YOU WANT, I'M DONE INDULGIN YOU. I'M NOT ANSWERIN ANY MORE OF YOUR STUPID TEXTS.

After hitting SEND, he waited, hoping the mystery texter would give up their little game. He didn't have to wait very long.

OH, U'LL KEEP ANSWERING MY TEXTS IF U DON'T WANT ANYTHING 2 HAPPEN 2 SWEET LIL' ROGER.

He reread the text a few times, his mouth went dry as if stuffed with cotton and the tips of his fingers felt numb. He had said he wasn't going to answer any more texts, and he'd meant it, but he couldn't ignore such a statement.

WHAT DOES ROGER HAVE TO DO WITH THIS?

A speedy reply. ROGER'S HERE WITH ME. UR GOING 2 DO EXACTLY WHAT I SAY OR HE MIGHT MEET WITH AN UNFORTUNATE ACCIDENT.

Stunned, as if he'd just been sucker-punched in the gut, Ethan scanned his surroundings again. No one seemed to be paying him any attention at the moment, and while he spotted plenty of people in the vicinity with cell phones stuck to their ears like permanent attachments, he couldn't see anyone texting. He turned back to his phone, which suddenly felt hot in his hand, and began a rapid-fire back and forth with the mystery texter.

IS THIS SOME KIND OF JOKE? IF SO, I DON'T THINK IT'S VERY FUNNY.

NO JOKE, MY FRIEND. UR SWEETIE IS RIGHT HERE NEXT 2 ME. U'VE NO IDEA JUST HOW STRONG DUCT TAPE IS.

I THINK YOU'VE WATCHED THE *SCREAM* MOVIES A FEW TOO MANY TIMES.

I WANT U TO GET UP AND HEAD TOWARD THE PUBLIC LIBRARY.

I'M NOT GOIN ANYWHERE.

U WILL, AND U WILL NOT ALERT THE AU-THORITIES, OR UR SWEETIE ROGER WILL SUFFER 4 IT.

YOU EXPECT ME TO BELIEVE THAT YOU HAVE ROGER? I'M NOT A FOOL.

U DOUBT ME?

I THINK YOU'RE A TOTAL CRACKPOT GET-TIN A KICK OUTTA MESSIN WITH ME.

FINE, WHY DON'T U CALL ROGER THEN? SEE WHAT'S HOLDING HIM UP?

Ninety percent sure this was all just a practical joke of some kind but with that nagging ten percent tying his stom-ach in knots, he quickly dialed Roger's cell phone number. Roger would answer, say he was stuck in traffic or had lost track of time, and everything would be—

From close behind him, he heard the familiar strains

of the George Michael song "Freedom,"; one of Roger's favorites and the ring tone of his phone. A smile blossoming on his face, Ethan turned around expecting to see Roger behind him. He must have somehow blocked his number and was just having a little fun.

Only, Roger wasn't there. No one was, and yet the song kept playing, somewhat muffled but definitely close. He stood slowly and walked toward the sound, honing in on it. It seemed to be coming from…that couldn't be right…it came from a large trashcan just outside the bistro's main entrance. Heedless of the stares he attracted, he dug through the refuse until he came up with a small black phone that he instantly recognized as Roger's because of the chip on one corner, where it had once been dropped and hit the side of the kitchen sink.

He disconnected his own phone, silencing George Michael. What did this prove, if anything? Roger loved his phone, was rarely without it; he certainly wouldn't have tossed it in the garbage, not even for a prank. Yet, this was Roger's phone…wasn't it? Ethan flipped it open and scrolled through the contacts, scanning the names of Roger's friends and co-workers, and there was Ethan's number.

Ethan's phone suddenly came to life in his left hand, thrumming with a new text, and the rapid fire began anew.

NOW R U READY 2 LISTEN?

WHAT ARE YOU PLAYIN AT YOU SONOFA-BITCH?

TEMPER, TEMPER! GETTING UPSET WON'T HELP POOR ROGER.

JUST TELL ME WHAT YOU WANT.

I ALREADY TOLD U, START WALKING WEST TOWARD THE PUBLIC LIBRARY.

Ethan looked back toward the outside tables, at the patrons, all laughing and chatting and enjoying their meals. He could go up to one of them, or better yet, use his phone to call the police.

But what if the mystery texter did have Roger? The phone in the trash certainly pointed toward that possibility, and the mystery texter had already proven he could see everything Ethan did. Trying to alert someone could get Roger hurt.

The phone vibrated again, startling him.

BE A GOOD BOY AND DO AS UR TOLD. START WALKING. HALFWAY BETWEEN HERE AND THE LIBRARY IS A NARROW ALLEY THAT RUNS BEHIND THE "KEEP IT CLEAN" LAUNDROMAT. GO DOWN IT.

With one last look toward his untouched second latte, which seemed to represent the rational world he'd somehow stepped out of, Ethan turned and started walking.

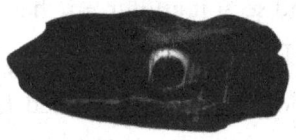

Six months later...

Roger sat at an outside table, even though the weather was really much too cold for that sort of thing. It wasn't snowing yet, but the forecast called for it, and his breath chugged out of his mouth in white puffs. He huddled over his coffee like a homeless man over a fire in a trash barrel. The patrons inside looked out at him as if he were mad, but the wait staff was used to him. He came by the bistro every day and sat at the same table.

This was the bistro where he was supposed to have met Ethan, where he had planned to tell Ethan that he would move in with him, the place where their new life together was set to begin. Only, he had arrived late and found Ethan already gone. The staff confirmed Ethan had been there, at this very table, but then had begun to act very peculiar and walked off.

No one had seen him since.

He couldn't help but feel responsible for Ethan's disappearance. If only he hadn't been late that day, but it really hadn't been his fault. He'd been on his way when some asshole bumped into him from behind and snatched his cell phone out of the little holster attached to his belt. A police officer across the street had seen it and given chase, but the thief had gotten away, and Roger had been stuck giving a statement. Without his phone, and with a decided lack of pay phones in the city in this cellular age, he'd been unable to call to let Ethan know he'd be late.

After initially finding Ethan gone from their meeting place, and away from his apartment, he had feared he'd blown it by making his boyfriend wait a week for an answer. He'd concluded that Ethan had tired of the indecision and made the decision himself. Roger had been more than prepared to beg Ethan's forgiveness and prove he wanted to be with him.

Only, he never got the chance. Ethan never returned to his apartment, never went back to his job. His friends and family never heard a word from him. No activity was reported on his bank account or credit cards. He'd simply vanished. Authorities had no clues, although Roger had the sinking feeling he was a suspect at first. Before long, Ethan's missing person's case got filed away with all the others that remained unsolved.

He had tried his own investigation at first, asking questions of the bistro staff, talking with regular customers who had been there that day. Everyone said Ethan had been doing a lot of texting, talking to himself, digging through the garbage, and looking generally distraught. Unfortunately, he was no detective and had run face-first into a dead end.

But Roger couldn't let go. If they'd found Ethan's body in an alley somewhere, beaten and lifeless, it would have been tragic, but he could have had closure and tried to move on. But this—the not knowing, the constant nagging questions, it was just too much. Ethan was gone, but he wasn't *gone*. Which was why he kept returning to this bistro, this table, the last place he knew for sure Ethan had been, as if they could somehow be together across time.

His thoughts were interrupted when the cell phone he'd bought to replace the stolen one started chirping from its holster. He plucked it from a pocket and saw a text from an UNKNOWN NUMBER. With a frown, he flipped open his phone and checked the message.

HELLO. HOW R U?

THE ELEVATOR GAME

Half a block from the O'Hara Building, Bobby's cell phone rang. He smiled when he saw his girlfriend's name on the Caller ID.

"Hey doll face," he said, stopping in front of O'Hara and leaning his head back to stare straight up the stone façade of the building. "What's shaking?"

"I just got your message about being a little late for dinner," Pauline said. "What's going on, working over?"

"No, just have an errand to run before heading home."

"What kind of errand?"

"I'd tell you, but you might not like it."

"Let me guess, you're stopping off for a quickie with that transvestite hooker who's always hanging out in the Piggly Wiggly parking lot," Pauline said in that dry deadpan tone of hers that never failed to make him laugh.

"No, Bernadette is a little out of my price range. Actually, I'm just outside the O'Hara Building downtown."

"The O'Hara Building? Nothing in there but lawyers and dentists. We're not married, so you can't be filing for divorce. I can only assume you're there looking to get a root canal."

"I'm here because this is the only building in town that's over ten stories tall."

"What's that got to do with…oh, wait, is this that weird thing you were reading about online last night?"

"The elevator game," Bobby said, stepping out of the flow of traffic on the sidewalk and taking a seat on a metal bench outside the building. "I can't get it out of my mind, I have to try it."

"Explain it to me again."

"I knew you weren't listening to me last night."

"It was almost midnight, I was half asleep."

"Well, the way it works is you have to find a building with at least ten floors, get in an elevator alone—*alone* is key—then you start going to specific floors in a certain order. Eventually a woman will get on the elevator with you on the fifth floor, or at least something that *looks* like a woman, but you aren't supposed to talk to her or even look directly at her. Once she joins you, you press the button for the ground floor but the elevator will instead take you to the tenth. If you've followed all the rules, when the doors open on the tenth floor you'll find yourself in some kind of alternate dimension."

A pause on the line, then, "That's the stupidest thing I've ever heard."

"This from the woman who won't say the name Bloody Mary into a mirror."

"Touché, but just to be clear, I don't really believe that a ghost is going to jump out of the mirror at me. You don't really believe you'll end up in another dimension…right?"

"I'm not a dumbbell. Of course I don't, but it's exciting to think about. The way it's exciting to think Bigfoot or the Loch Ness monster might be real."

"Maybe we have different ideas of excitement."

"You read your Mary Higgins Clark novels, and I'll do this."

"So any idea how long you'll be visiting this alternate dimension? I want to know when to start dinner."

"Shouldn't be long. I'll see you in a bit, will regale you with tales of the other side."

Pauline's throaty laugh trilled through the phone. "Love ya, nut."

"Love you too."

After disconnecting the call, Bobby used the phone to Google "rules for playing the elevator game". Once he had the instructions on hand, he pushed open the glass door to the O'Hara Building and stepped into the small lobby area with the faux-marble floors and potted palms. A reception desk stood against the wall to the left, but it was currently unmanned. However, a directory of all the offices in the building hung on the wall above the desk. Bobby gave this only a cursory glance as he wasn't here to see anyone in particular. His only appointment was with the tenth floor.

The building had two elevators located side by side in a small alcove to his right. An older gentleman with white whiskers and a dark blue suit stood with his hands clasped behind his back, waiting for one of the cars. Bobby joined him, reaching out and pressing the "Up" button, even though it was already lit.

With a soft *ding*, the doors to the left-hand elevator slid open. The man in the suit entered then turned facing back out into the alcove. Bobby remained where he was, and when the doors began to close, the man held out a hand to stop them, giving Bobby an inquisitive look.

"No thanks," Bobby said. "I'll wait for the next one."

The man frowned, removing his hand and letting the doors glide shut.

Bobby waited another half a minute before the doors to his right opened. The car was empty so he stepped inside, consulted the instructions on his phone, then pushed the button for the fourth floor. Once the doors closed again, the lift started to rise.

A nervous fluttering began in Bobby's gut, and a tingling spread across his skin. A feeling he associated with horror movies watched late at night with all the lights out. He had told Pauline the truth, he didn't really expect to find himself in another world, but the idea that such a thing might be possible gave him a thrill and a chill. Like playing with a Ouija board. You don't really imagine that you will make contact with a spirit, but just entertaining the notion is exciting and fun.

The elevator arrived on the fourth floor. Bobby tensed, half hoping no one would enter the elevator and ruin his game, and half hoping someone would. The corridor was deserted so he pressed the button for the second floor, soon traveling downward again.

After a brief stop before heading up to the sixth floor, Bobby glanced at the security camera in the top right corner of the elevator car, wondering how he might look to anyone watching the footage. A grown man of 36, dressed in faded jeans and a ratty AC/DC T-shirt, riding up and down in the elevator as part of some childish game.

Well, wouldn't be the first time he'd been called childish. Pauline had even used that one on him a time or two. He didn't care. Just because you got older, didn't mean you had to lose your sense of whimsy and silliness. That was the stuff that kept you young at heart.

Thus the spooky elevator game, making him feel like a teenager walking through a cemetery after dark just to give himself the willies.

After the sixth floor, Bobby returned to the second, then rose all the way to the tenth. No one else entered the elevator on any of these floors. Considering that it was after five and most of the offices in the building would be closed by now, this wasn't all that surprising, but the superstitious part of Bobby's brain whispered that there was some force at work ensuring he had the car to himself. A delicious thread of unease coiled around his spine like a snake, delighting him.

This only lasted until the elevator descended from the tenth floor to the fifth. When the doors *whooshed* open this time, he found someone waiting in the corridor. Not just someone, but someone he knew. His surprise was so total that it took him a few seconds to find his voice. "Pauline, what are you doing here?"

She wore a simple white blouse and fitted black shirt that stopped mid-shin, her chestnut brown hair pulled into a ponytail that draped over one shoulder. Her eyes were hidden behind an oversized pair of Audrey Hepburn sunglasses. As the doors began to close, she quickly stepped into the elevator, then turned to face the front.

"Decided to join me, doll face?" he said with a grin. "See, it's fun to creep yourself out. Want to hit the button for the ground level?"

Pauline did not move, did not even glance in his direction. With a shrug, Bobby leaned past her and pressed the button that would take them back to the lobby.

"You must have really hauled ass to get here so quick," he said. "You're awfully dressy for an elevator ride. If you want me to take you out somewhere fancy for dinner, we'll have to swing back by the apartment first. I'm not exactly dressed for it."

Still Pauline said nothing, staring straight ahead at the elevator doors. Bobby opened his mouth to ask her what was wrong, then shut his mouth abruptly as he noticed something wrong himself. The elevator was moving again, but not down. Up.

With a frown, he pressed the button for the first floor again, but the car continued to rise.

According to the instruction for the elevator game, after the fifth floor you would press the button for the ground level but the elevator would instead take you to the tenth.

"Something strange is going on," he said, starting to jab the lobby button repeatedly. When it had no effect, he pressed the buttons for several other floors until the entire panel was lit up. Still the elevator made its inexorable way skyward.

Bobby laughed, but the sound had a brittle edginess to it. "Must be some kind of malfunction. Or maybe it's some quirk of the mechanics of an elevator, that if you go to certain floors in a certain order, it automatically takes you to the tenth floor. That could be how the whole elevator game thing got started. You think?"

No response from Pauline. Her stillness was almost preternatural.

"Hello!" he shouted, placing his hands to his mouth like a bullhorn. "Did you come all the way downtown just to give me the silent treatment?"

Still nothing.

Bobby began waving his hands in front of her covered eyes and snapping his fingers by her ears. "What's the matter with you? You trying to scare me or something? What are you supposed to be, some kind of—"

His words cut off abruptly as he recalled more of the instructions for the elevator game. On the fifth floor a woman would enter that you weren't supposed to talk to or look at, and from there the elevator would take you to the tenth floor.

Could it be...

No, of course not. This wasn't just "a woman"; this was Pauline...wasn't it?

His thoughts were interrupted by a soft *ding*. His eyes darted to the numbers above the elevator doors. They had reached the tenth floor.

The doors opened onto a dark corridor. All the hall lights were extinguished, though a sickly yellow glow seemed to emanate from somewhere down the hall, lending the air a quality of dirty dishwater.

"Was there a power outage?" he muttered as he stepped past Pauline then realized that was impossible since the elevator was still working. He reached the threshold but hesitated to step out of the car and into the corridor.

"Where are you going?" said a voice from behind him. A voice that sounded like Pauline's and yet didn't at the same time. More gravelly, as if she were gargling pebbles.

He turned slowly to face her. She had not moved, except now her lips curled slightly in an enigmatic smile. The glow from the hallway touched her skin, giving it a jaundiced look.

With a trembling hand, Bobby reached out for the sunglasses. Not being able to see her eyes unsettled him more than he could explain. He pulled them off her face, expecting to see her baby blues, hoping that she would break into laughter and exclaim, "Gotcha!"

But what he saw behind those sunglasses sent such a jolt of terror through his body that he wasn't even aware of his bladder letting go and the front of his pants dampening. There was nothing behind those glasses. No eyes, just bottomless pits of soul-sucking darkness with distant points of red light deep within.

A scream building in his throat, Bobby scuttled backward. His right foot left the elevator car, but instead of finding the floor of the corridor, it found nothing.

He fell back.

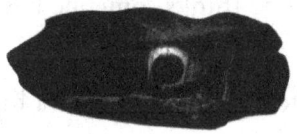

Pauline sat in a small conference room on the third floor of the police station downtown, staring at the laptop open before her. The picture on the screen was a bit grainy and in black and white, but she could clearly make out Bobby. He stood in the elevator, rocking on the balls of his feet like he did whenever they had to wait in line at the movies. Once he looked directly up at the camera with a shy, embarrassed grin.

She felt as if she might throw up…again. She'd thrown up twice already, once at the apartment right after getting the call and then once at the morgue where she'd identified what was left of the body. She felt completely hollowed out, as if her body were nothing more than an empty bag inflated with hot air.

Detective Sanchez leaned over her shoulder and pointed at the screen. "This is where things take a weird turn, when he gets to the fifth floor."

The footage showed the elevator doors opening on a deserted corridor and then closing again. Though Bobby was still alone, he suddenly became animated and appeared to be talking while staring off to his left. Pauline hunched over closer to the laptop.

"There's no sound," Sanchez said. "No idea what he's

saying, but it's like he thinks someone has joined him in the car."

On the screen, Bobby pushed a button on the panel then continued talking, gesturing casually. He paused, then pressed a button on the panel again. Another pause and then he began pushing buttons wildly, seemingly at random. He continued talking, then placed his hands up to his lips as if shouting, followed by frantic waving of his hands and snapping of his fingers. The sight was so bizarre it made the skin on Pauline's arms seize up in gooseflesh.

The elevator stopped and the doors opened onto the tenth floor corridor. Bobby moved slowly and cautiously forward then stopped and turned back around. He reached out and seemed to pluck something right out of the air, though his hands were empty. Even with the poor resolution, Pauline could not mistake the mask of terror that twisted his features and a dark stain spreading at the crotch of his pants. His mouth gaped and he scurried back into the corridor, turning and disappearing to the right.

Sanchez reached over and hit the spacebar, pausing the footage. "That's where it happened," he said. "He ran straight down the hallway, crashed through the window that led onto the fire-escape, and went over the railing. Ten stories down. A janitor witnessed the whole thing."

The room seemed to spin around Pauline, and she gripped the edge of the table to keep from flying off into space.

The emptiness inside her was beginning to fill with pain like jagged glass, and she found herself wishing for the hollowness again.

Sanchez sat in the chair next to her. "After watching that, are you still maintaining that your boyfriend wasn't on anything?"

"Bobby didn't do drugs," she said vehemently. "Maybe he smoked a little weed back in high school, but not for years."

"Maybe he had a problem you didn't know about?"

"I've lived with the man for five years. If he was on drugs, I think I'd know it."

"You'd be surprised how well addicts can hide things from people. Even those closest to them."

"I know Bobby better than I know myself," she said, inwardly wincing as she realized she would have to get accustomed to using past tense. "I'm a hundred percent certain he wasn't on drugs."

And yet the image of him talking to no one, waving his arms and snapping his fingers for no apparent reason, made her question her own conviction.

Sanchez spread his hands and said, "Well, the toxicology report will tell us for sure, but I don't know how to explain this if it isn't drugs. You say he had no history of mental instability?"

"No."

"Any schizophrenics in his family?"

231

"No. I mean, I don't think so. Not that he ever mentioned."

Sanchez put a hand over one of hers and, his expression softening, said, "I know this is rough on you, but we're just trying to make sense of this. You say that when you talked to him on the phone earlier, he sounded normal?"

"Yes. He was joking and laughing, just wanted to play that stupid game he read about on the net."

"The elevator game?"

Pauline nodded, her lips pressed tightly together as another bout of nausea threatened. Only this time she was afraid everything would come spewing forth. Organs, bones, muscles, until she was turned completely inside out.

"I think we're done," Sanchez said quietly. "Go on home, try to get some rest. If we have any further questions, we'll contact you."

She nodded again, pushing herself up on unsteady legs. Sanchez offered his hand but she turned away, stumbling out the door. Leaning against the wall for a moment, she felt tears sting her eyes and dribble sluggishly down her cheeks. She knew people were staring at her, but she didn't care. Everything had the surreal quality of a nightmare, and even though she knew she was wide awake, she preferred to hold on to the illusion that this was a dream. Then none of it had to be real.

With a shaky breath she started down the corridor. At

the elevator she paused briefly, considering, before moving on. She'd take the stairs.

THE PIGMALION PIGS

Joe came back into the living room to find Tasha stretched out on the sofa, watching a cooking competition show on TV. Joe lifted her legs, dropped onto the cushion, and settled his wife's feet on his lap.

"Julie get to sleep okay?" Tasha asked, wiggling her toes.

Joe recognized this as her nonverbal way of asking for a foot rub, so he started kneading her soles, causing her to purr softly. "Yeah, she was out before I even got halfway through the book."

"What did you read her tonight?"

"Something called *The Mouse and the Motorcycle*."

"That sounds fun."

"She liked it when I made the engine revving sounds."

"I think it's so wonderful that you read to her every night. That way, when she's old enough to read herself, she'll already have an appreciation for books."

"Exactly. Then I won't have to worry about her spending hour after hour staring blankly at stupid reality TV shows."

Tasha tore her eyes away from the screen then playfully kicked at her husband. "Hey, that's not nice. This is quality entertainment. Look, that chef has to cook with a potato masher duct taped to his hand."

"I stand corrected. I didn't realize how intellectual this show is."

The two shared a laugh. This type of teasing was familiar territory between them, Tasha's love of television and Joe's aversion to the medium. Ironic, considering he worked for the local NBC affiliate, WYFF 4, albeit in the marketing department.

"You know," Joe said during the commercial break, when he knew he had a better chance of getting his wife's full attention, "I was thinking about my favorite book when I was Julie's age."

"*Encyclopedia Brown?*"

"No, it was called *The Pigmalion Pigs.*"

"I don't think I've ever heard of that one. Then again, I didn't grow up in a household that had many books in it. Lots of alcohol, but not so much with the books."

"It was about this family of pigs. Percy and Priscilla

Pigmalion, and their children Peter and Patty. Patty Pigmalion was kind of shy and bookish, but one day she got invited to this big party that everyone in school was going to and she was worried about looking like a big nerd. Her family banded together and gave her a makeover; a fancy new dress, make-up, stunning hairdo, the whole nine yards."

"Ah, thus the Pygmalion part."

"Yes, though I wasn't familiar with that term at the time. The book actually had a great message about being yourself, because when she got to the party all the other kids were put off by her new look and said they had liked her the way she was. So she changed into some sweats, scrubbed off the make-up and mussed up her hair, and everybody had a great time."

"That's sweet."

"Yeah, I bet Julie would really get a kick out of it. I wonder if it's still in print."

Leaning forward, he snagged the iPad from the coffee table and opened Amazon. In the search engine he typed "Pigmalion Pigs".

DID YOU MEAN: *Pygmalion Pigs*?

Joe frowned, certain he'd used the correct spelling for the book, but he clicked the link and sat for a moment staring at the cover image that appeared.

It was just as he remembered from his childhood. Percy, Priscilla, and Peter standing around little Patty who was resplendent in a sparkly blue dress, her hair swept up onto of her head with a string of pearls resting atop the bun like a tiara, and bright red lipstick on her snout. Exactly the way he saw it in his memory...

...except for the title at the top.

The Pygmalion Pigs.

"They changed it."

"What?" Tasha asked, having gotten immersed in her program again.

"They changed the spelling of the book's title." He held up the tablet for her to see.

"It looks right to me."

"It is right, and that's why it's wrong. Originally they spelled it with an I after the P, not a Y."

"That's misspelled," she said.

"I know, but they were playing off the word pig. Get it?"

"Of course I get it, but what I'm saying is, maybe they started to worry that it wasn't setting a good example for kids, having a misspelling right in the title like that."

Joe glanced back at the image on the screen. "I guess that could be it."

"What's wrong? You've suddenly got your down-in-the-dumps face."

"I don't know, it's just...I mean, it's silly, but seeing that they altered the title is like seeing your favorite childhood playground turned into a parking lot or your childhood home demolished."

Tasha giggled, sat up and gave him a peck on the cheek. "I love you, but you can be all kinds of melodramatic sometimes."

Joe found himself laughing as well. "In any case, with an I or a Y, I think Julie will love it."

And Joe clicked ORDER NOW.

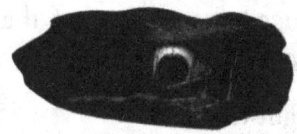

It was after six when Joe got home from the station. He stepped inside, sat his briefcase in the foyer, loosened his tie, and went down the hallway, through the swinging door, and into the kitchen.

Tasha stood at the stove, working on supper. Julie sat in her booster seat at the table, coloring. Actually, she merely scribbled all over the page with a red crayon. When she saw her father standing there, she squealed, dropping the crayon and holding her arms out. Joe picked her up and kissed her on the top of the head. He knew he was biased, but he thought she was the most adorable four-year-old in the world.

"Hey, honey," Tasha said, not looking up from the boiling pot on the burner. Joe wasn't sure what she was making, but it smelled delicious. "How was your day?"

"Can't complain. How about you?"

"Upstairs toilet was clogged. Took me an hour and a drain snake to fix it. Turns out Julie flushed one of her dolls."

"You wouldn't do a thing like that…would you?" he said to the girl, scrunching up his face in mock seriousness. Julie giggled and buried her face in his chest.

"A package came for you today," Tasha said, pointing toward the counter. "It's from Amazon."

"Awesome, it must be my little surprise for Julie."

"For me," the girl said, her little hands gripping Joe's shoulders.

"That's right, for you."

"Are you sure she deserves a treat after clogging the toilet?" Tasha asked.

"I be good, Mommy, I promise."

Tasha looked at the girl with a titled head. "I don't know, I noticed someone had toys strewn all over the living room."

"I go clean them up right now," the girl said, squirming to get down. Joe placed her on the floor and she took off like a wind-up toy, pushing through the door and making a beeline for the living room.

"Jesus," Joe said. "She's so excited, I'm afraid it will be a huge disappointment when she discovers her surprise is just a book."

Tasha returned to the stove. "She loves story time with Daddy. She'll be absolutely delighted."

Joe stepped to the counter and picked up the package, opening it and letting the thin, oversized book slide out into his hands. That familiar cover, but the not-quite-right title. "You want to hear something strange?"

"The stranger, the better."

"I got online at work to research this book."

"That is strange," Tasha said. "Using your work time to research a children's story."

"That's not the strange part. I wanted to find out when exactly they altered the title's spelling."

"And what did you find out?"

"Nothing."

"What do you mean?"

"I mean every single reference I found about the book has Pygmalion spelled with a Y, and I can't find anything about the title ever being changed. In fact, I found some images of old copies that are spelled with a Y, none with an I."

"Hmm," she said, tasting the stew that bubbled in the pot.

"That's all you have to say? Hmm?"

"What do you want me to say? You just remembered it wrong."

"No, I didn't. That was my favorite book from the time I was four until I was in second grade. I still had the thing when I finally moved out of my parents' house at twenty-one. I'm telling you it was Pigmalion with an I."

"Honey, I'm not doubting your mental prowess, but you were a kid, and with the story being about pigs, you probably just got that all jumbled up in your memory."

"I remember that cover vividly."

Tasha stood with her head tilted again, the same skeptical look she always gave Julie when she thought the girl was being less than honest. "What then? You think someone methodically went through the net and rewrote the history of a children's book?"

Joe laughed, although the sound was somewhat forced. "I know, it's just weird is all."

"Memory is weird. Growing up, I heard people tell the story of how my sister Violet got her big toe cut off in a bicycle chain when she was six so often that I truly believed I remembered being there and seeing it happened, even though I wasn't born for another year."

"I know you're right," Joe said, though a tingle of unease still lingered in his gut.

"I always am. Now go wash up, supper will be ready in about ten minutes."

Joe kissed his wife, then slid the book back into the package so Julie wouldn't see it on his way upstairs.

Julie cuddled under the comforter, her head dimpling the plush pillow. Joe sat on the edge of the bed by her feet, the book open in his lap. He read to her in a soft tone, changing his voice for the various characters. He thought his daughter was enjoying the story; she giggled in all the appropriate places and the expression on her face could only be described as enraptured.

For that matter, Joe was pretty enraptured himself. Despite the simplicity of the story, he found himself really enjoying it. He realized most of this was pure nostalgia, but he thought the story was full of charm and warmth and humor, and he was so glad to be able to share this part of his own childhood with Julie.

He turned to the final page. Patty had just arrived at the party, which was attended by a menagerie of animal children—dogs and cats and horses and cows and squirrels and porcupines. Something seemed a bit off about the illustration, but Joe wasn't really focused on the picture. He read along.

"'A hush fell over the room as everyone froze, staring at Patty. She felt like she was under a microscope. Finally Gina Giraffe stepped forward, bending down her long neck to look Patty over. Then Gina exclaimed, "Oh Patty, I simply *love* your new look!" Everyone at the party exploded into cheers. Patty felt like crying as the wave of acceptance washed over—'"

"Daddy, why'd you stop?"

Joe looked up at his daughter, then let his gaze drop back to the page, rereading the words over and over, expecting them to rearrange themselves into something that made sense. Yet they stubbornly remained the same.

"Daddy!" Julie said again, sitting up. "Finish the story."

He stuttered for a moment before finally finishing the rest. "'Patty felt like crying as the wave of acceptance washed over her. Finally she was one of the gang, no longer an outcast or a freak. With a smile on her snout, she joined the party and had a great time.'"

"Yay!" Julie exclaimed. "I'm glad everybody likes her now that she's like them."

Joe closed the book, staring down at the cover and the title that was misspelled by being spelled correctly. "You know, you don't have to be like everybody else for them to like you. You can be your own person, and that's good enough."

Julie shrugged and settled back onto the pillow. "Thank you for the story, Daddy. It was good."

"Yeah, you get some sleep, sweetie."

Joe kissed his daughter on the forehead, turned out the lamp by her bed, leaving the nightlight plugged into an outlet across the room glowing softly. He stepped out into the hall and closed the door halfway then walked back to the living room. He felt detached, not quite in his body, as if his soul were attached by a tether, bobbing along just above and behind him.

Tasha sat cross-legged on the floor between the sofa and coffee table, working on one of her thousand-piece puzzles. She collected puzzles but rarely worked on them, stacking them up in the hall closet to form teetering towers. Normally he would have wondered if she'd pulled one out tonight just to prove some point about how she wasn't addicted to TV and could stop at any time, but his mind was on other matters at the moment.

"They rewrote it," he said, tossing the book on the table, causing the puzzle pieces to jump and a few to fall onto the carpet.

Tasha gave him an annoyed look and started picking up the fallen pieces. "What?"

"The book, it has a different ending. Now instead of the kids telling her she didn't have to change for them, they are all happy she changed, makes it seem like that was the only way she'd be able to fit in."

Tasha picked up the book and started flipping through it. "That's a terrible message to send kids."

"And it's not the original ending," he said, taking a seat on the sofa. "I know you think I'm just misremembering the spelling of the title, but I am positive how that book ended and this is different."

After placing the book back on the table, Tasha looked up at her husband with one eyebrow raised and a small smile curling the corners of her mouth.

"What's that look for?" he asked.

"Nothing. It's just that…well, you're starting to sound a little bit like one of those nutty conspiracy theorists."

"Are you saying I don't know how my favorite childhood story ends? One of my first memories is of my mother sitting by my bed reading the damn thing to me."

Tasha held up her hands in surrender, but there was steel in her eyes when she said, "Hey, don't yell at me, I'm just saying you're getting a little obsessive over this."

Joe opened his mouth to say he wasn't yelling when he realized his voice was louder and more strident than he'd intended. He took a deep breath before resuming. "I'm sorry. This whole thing is just really weird."

"Do you think it's possible your mother didn't like the ending and made up one she thought had a better message, and that's the one you remember?"

Joe shook his head. "No, after I learned to read, I started reading it myself. Read it so much the pages started falling out and my mother had to tape them back in."

Tasha shrugged, reminding him of little Julie who had picked up a lot of her mother's body language. "Maybe they thought the original ending was too old-fashioned and they changed it to be more in line with the times. Call it *Breakfast Club* Syndrome."

"*Breakfast Club* Syndrome?"

"Yeah, remember in the movie *The Breakfast Club*, Ally Sheedy's goth character had to completely change her look in order to get Emilio Estevez."

Joe laughed, and it felt good. "You have a very interesting way of looking at the world, you know that?"

"So I've been told. Now if you'll excuse me, I have about 997 pieces of this puzzle that I still have to put together. Want to help?"

"I could…or we could watch *Project Runway*."

"Well, if you're going to twist my arm," Tasha said, already swiping the pieces back into the box.

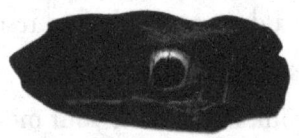

When Joe came home the next evening, Tasha was waiting in the foyer with her arms crossed over her chest, her lips a stern slash of red. He'd been expecting this.

"Evening, sweetie," he said with a forced smile.

"Where have you been? I've been calling and texting you for the last two hours."

"Sorry, I turned my cell off."

"I called the station, and Jeff said that you left early today."

"Don't worry, I wasn't having an affair or anything."

"Just tell me where you were."

"I went to the library, then stopped by all the used bookstores in town to see if I could find any old copies of *The Pigmalion Pigs*."

Tasha paused a moment then said, "I'd rather you were having an affair."

"You're funny."

"I'm not joking. You're obsessed with this thing. It's starting to seem OCD or something."

"I just wanted to see what I could find."

"And?"

"Well, I located two copies of the book that were published in the '60s. Both spelled Pygmalion with a Y and had the ending where the kids love Patty's new look."

"Then that settles it, you were mistaken."

"I guess," Joe said, beating his briefcase against his leg.

Tasha rolled her eyes. "What more proof do you need?"

"I don't know, but I'm positive that the copy I had when I was a kid was different."

"Maybe you're losing your mind."

Joe sputtered a laugh. "That's entirely possible. What's for dinner?"

"Spaghetti. The garlic bread is almost done."

"Okay, I'm going to do a couple of emails for work, then I'll set the table."

Tasha's expression softened slightly and she gave him a peck on the cheek.

He headed into the living room where Julie sat on the floor playing with her Barbies. She had arranged them in a circle.

"Hey munchkin," he said, reaching down to pinch one of her plump cheeks. "You and your dolls having a party?"

"Yes, Daddy. You wanna be invited?"

"Thanks, but this looks like an all-girls kind of shindig. I'll just be over on the sofa if your friends get rowdy and you need a bouncer."

Julie giggled as if she understood what her father was talking about then turned back to her dolls.

Joe took a seat and pulled the iPad from his briefcase. Instead of going to his email, he opened a search engine and typed "Pigmalion Pigs name change." Several articles appeared, but one in particular caught his interest, because it was from a website entitled Proof of Other Realities. Joe clinked the link and started reading.

"*The children's book* The Pygmalion Pigs *is considered by many to be compelling evidence of the existence of alternate realities. This website recently conducted an informal poll and found that four out of ten people remember the book's title being spelled* The Pigmalion Pigs. *Some even stated that they remember the story unfolding differently. And yet there is no evidence that the book ever appeared in any other form than it does now, with the title spelled* The Pygmalion Pigs. *Some of those polled said they dug up their childhood copies and were surprised to find the spelling was even changed on those. What is most fascinating about this case is that it not only suggests the existence of parallel universes, but it suggests that we can shift from one to the other throughout our lives."*

Joe was still reading when the tablet was suddenly snatched from his hands. Tasha looked at the screen, then turned her withering gaze on him. "I knew you weren't doing work emails."

"I was. I mean, I was going to, I just—"

"Get out of this house."

"What?"

"Didn't you tell me once that your parents still have a bunch of your childhood toys boxed up in their basement?"

"Yeah, I think so."

"Then there's a chance that book is there as well. Hop in your car and head over there."

"Now? That's crazy."

"Yes, which is exactly how you've been acting. This is just going to continue eating at your mind until you do this. Please, for your sake and mine, go."

Joe made a show of debating the issue with himself

before rising from the couch and kissing his wife. "Thanks, sweetie, I won't be long."

"Well, to what do I owe the pleasure of an unexpected visit from my baby boy?" Joe's mother said as she greeted him at the door.

"Mom, I called you fifteen minutes ago and told you I was on my way."

She stood aside and let him into the den, where his father sat in a recliner, watching TV. He glanced over and raised a hand to his son, then returned his focus to the tube.

"Yes," his mother said, "but it's very unusual for you to come calling so late, and just to go rummaging through some old boxes."

"I told you, I really think Julie will get a kick out of some of my old picture books from when I was a kid."

"And you had to rush right over? It couldn't wait?"

"I wanted to get to it before it slipped my mind."

The two of them walked through the archway into the kitchen, leaving his father bathed in the glow of the TV.

"Have you eaten?" his mother asked, opened the oven door and peered inside. The familiar aroma of roasted chicken wafted on the air. "I can fix you a plate."

"Tasha is keeping some spaghetti warm for me. Besides, this will only take a few minutes."

"Okay, you be careful. It's probably crawling with spiders down there."

As Joe opened the door to the basement and started down the narrow stairs, he couldn't help but smile. His mother had few fears—at 60 she went skydiving for the first time—but she couldn't abide spiders.

The basement was a small square with a concrete floor, the air musty and full of dust. Spider webs dangled from the low ceiling like old, forgotten party decorations. To the right were the washer and dryer, straight ahead stood an old work bench that his father used to tinker with home repairs. Currently, a toaster was strewn across the top in several pieces. Stacked against the wall to the left were about a dozen cardboard boxes.

Working by the harsh light of the overhead florescent tubes, Joe began opening the boxes one by one. He found old dresses that had belonged to his mother, a box of his father's bowling trophies from when he was in a league, broken knickknacks and chipped china, faded photos and old birthday cards.

He'd gone through half the boxes when he finally hit pay dirt.

He pulled back the flaps of a ripped box with water

stains on the top and the first thing he saw was He-Man and Luke Skywalker tangled together in a somewhat obscene knot of plastic and sculpted muscle. He tossed them aside and began pawing through more of his past—action figures and matchbox cars and toy guns and yo-yos. At the very bottom of the box were several pictures books, some Seuss and *Amelia Bedelia* and *Babar*. All these he discarded, they could be incinerated for all he cared. He was interested in only one book, and it had to be—

He moved aside a copy of *Dandelion* and caught a glimpse of Patty in her new dress. Joe snatched up the book, an idiot grin spread across his face. The book was tattered and discolored, several of the pages falling out to sift down like autumn leaves. He glanced at the front cover, preparing for vindication as he read the title.

The Pygmalion Pigs.

The grin withering to a tense frown, Joe quickly flipped to the last page of the book. The image showed all the animals at the party cheering and laughing and dancing, with Patty in her new dress at the center.

"No, no, no, this is all wrong."

Joe experienced a moment of vertigo, a woozy lightheadedness overcoming him, and his voice echoed in his own ears. He reached out to the wall to steady himself, but gasped and jerked his hand back when he realized the wall was no longer in front of him.

Instead, he saw a reflection of the room, as if the bricks had become a mirror. He stared at his own face, a dumbfounded expression making him look like one of the mentally handicapped children that lived in the group home on Wellington Street. He crouched there, frozen for a moment, and then watched himself sneeze, lose his balance, and fall onto his bottom.

And yet he hadn't sneezed, he hadn't lost his balance, he hadn't fallen over. It was only his reflection who had done that.

Joe bolted to his feet, and so did his reflection. Only at a slower pace. "What the hell is going on?" he and his doppelgänger said at the same time, creating that curious doubling effect again.

Joe reached up and scratched his chin as the reflection ran his fingers through his hair. "Am I dreaming?" the double said, closing his eyes. His voice had the same timbre and inflection as Joe's own. A perfect imitation.

"This isn't real," Joe said with a laugh as brittle as cracked ice. "Maybe Tasha's right, maybe I'm losing my mind."

The doppelgänger's eyes snapped open. "Tasha? What do you know about Tasha?"

"She's my wife," Joe said, thinking, *Why am I talking to myself?*

The reflection looked down at the book in his hands. "I don't understand what's happening. I just wanted to come find this book, to see if the title was spelled the way I remembered it."

Joe glanced down at the book in his own hands. "Pygmalion with a Y?"

"No, that's the way it *should be*, that's the way I remember it, but every copy including this one has Pigmalion spelled with an I."

"That's the way I remember it, but on every copy here it's spelled with a Y."

Joe found himself thinking of the article he'd read earlier, all that nonsense about parallel universes and alternate realities. At least it had seemed like nonsense at the time, but now that he was staring at the mirror image of himself, he started to wonder. And he could tell by the look in the doppelgänger's eyes that he was wondering the same thing.

"Maybe we should switch," the double said.

Joe frowned. "What?"

"Books, maybe we should switch books. You have the one I remember from childhood, I have the one you remember. Maybe we should just switch back."

"Can we do that? Is it possible?"

"I don't know how any of this is possible. Maybe because we're in the exact same place at the exact same time for the exact some reason. Maybe that opened some kind of, I don't know, *window* or something."

Taking shuffling, hesitant steps, Joe approached the

line of boxes that separated this basement from the identical one that existed across some unknowable gulf of time and space. His hand trembled as he held out the book, his double doing the same. Would they encounter resistance, an invisible wall? Would the air ripple like water or sizzle with electricity?

Joe didn't experience any of that, but he did notice a low hum in his ears. Not the buzz of an electrical current, but more like a hive of bees. Vertigo overcame him again and he swayed on his feet. The room seemed to spin. He thought he was falling, but then the spell passed and he was standing in his parents' basement, staring at the blank wall.

No doppelgänger, no reflection of the room. Just the wall.

"We didn't even get to switch bo—" he started, but then glanced at the cover.

The Pigmalion Pigs.

Quickly he flipped to the last page, where Gina Giraffe tells Patty Pigmalion that she didn't have to change for anyone, that everyone at the party had liked her just the way she was.

"Yes! Now I can prove to Tasha that I'm not crazy."

Without bothering to place the items he'd unpacked back in the boxes, he started up the staircase. Halfway to the top he became aware of the roaring sound of rain hitting the roof, and when he came up into the dark kitchen lightning flared bright through the windows. The air held the acrid stench of something burned. Apparently his mother had cooked the roast a little too long.

He turned to head through the archway and almost collided with his father. "Oh, sorry, Pop."

"Find what you were looking for down there?" the man asked with an amiable smile.

Joe held up the book. "Sure did."

"Want to split a frozen pizza?"

"No thanks, Tasha's waiting."

His father's fuzzy eyebrows rose up. "You're eating with Tasha and Julie tonight?"

Joe opened his mouth to ask why his father sounded so surprised when thunder rocked the house. "Jesus, this storm just rolled in out of nowhere."

"You feeling all right, son? It's been raining all day."

A chill spread all over Joe's skin, and he found himself staring at the book again, and the sight of the title now restored to coincide with his memory made him shiver. "Um, I need to go, Pop." He went into the den, which was quiet and empty. "Tell Mom I love her and I'll call tomorrow."

Hand on the doorknob, he glanced back to see his father frozen in the center of the room, his body shaking as tears rolled down his face.

"Pop, what's wrong?"

"Do you think you're funny?" the old man said in a deep, husky voice that Joe had never heard before. As if his father's body was now inhabited by a stranger.

"What are you talking about?"

"Son, I know you've been having a rough time lately, but that is no excuse for you to be so cruel."

"I really don't know—"

"Just get out of here," his father said, then turned to the right and disappeared down the hall that led to the bedrooms. Joe considered going after him, but he had a sinking feeling that he needed to get home as soon as possible.

The rain came in a torrent, impacting the earth with such force that each drop splashed back up like a mini explosion. As if to compliment this image, thunder crashed loud enough to cause the windows of the house to rattle, and lighting illuminated the sky in an atomic flash.

Joe was drenched within thirty seconds of stepping outside, but still he paused on the front walk, staring at the spot where he'd parked his Honda Fit when he first arrived. The car was gone, and in its place was a beat-up Pontiac Sunfire with a bent antenna.

He didn't understand what was happening. At least, he didn't want to understand. Reaching into his pocket for his keys, he discovered not the fob for the Fit but instead a plain metal key with Pontiac written on it.

The urgency to get home reaching a fever pitch, he jumped in the unfamiliar car, tossing the wet book on the passenger's seat, and backed quickly out into the street. The drive back to his house usually took half an hour, but despite the horrible weather conditions, Joe made the trip in half that time.

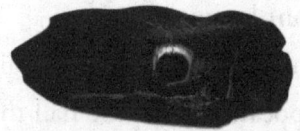

He skidded to a stop at the curb, not bothering to pull into the garage. The control for the automatic door wasn't hooked to the visor in this car anyway. Not bothering to close the car door but taking the time to grab the copy of *The Pigmalion Pigs*, he splashed through a puddle deep enough to drown a chihuahua, and bounded to the door.

Once he was on the porch and out of the relentless rain, he fumbled with his keys, shifting through them to find the one for the front door. He noticed he had fewer keys than usual, and the house key was not among them. He went through them four times to be sure. With a growl of frustration, he pounded on the door with a fist.

"Tasha! Tasha, open up, it's me! I must have lost my key!"

The storm was moving on, the rain slackening and the thunder and lightning fading, but twilight had descended, lending the neighborhood a shadowy gloom that filled him with a sense of foreboding.

Five minutes after he started knocking, the porch light buzzed to life and the door opened. Just a crack, and the security chain was still attached. Tasha's face, strained and pensive, peered out from the opening. "What do you want, Joe?"

"What do you think I want? I want to come in and get out of these wet clothes. I lost my key."

"Are you drunk?"

"No, I'm not drunk, I was just over at my folks' house looking for this," he said, holding up the waterlogged book.

"Jesus, Joe, are you still going on about that book? You need to see a shrink."

"Look at the spelling, Tash. Pigmalion with an I."

"Yes, just the way it has always been. Now maybe you'll stop with all this nonsense about how it used to be spelled with a Y."

Joe let his arms drop, as well as his mental defenses. Realization finally sunk it. Crazy as it sounded, he and the doppelgänger had exchanged more than just books.

"Maybe I'll read this to Julie tonight," he said.

Tasha barked a harsh laugh, glaring at him with a coldness he'd never witnessed before. "You know good and well you don't have her again until next weekend."

"Have her? No, this isn't right. This is where I belong. Let me come in and we can talk."

"Found a job yet?" Tasha asked.

"What? A job? WYFF—"

"The station laid you off almost a year ago. It's time you gave up on this idea that they're going to ask you back. Those unemployment checks aren't going to keep coming forever. Grow up, find another job, maybe then you can get your own place and move out of your father's house."

"Wait, I live with Pop?"

Tasha sighed and let her head hang down as if she hadn't the energy to hold it up any longer. "Go home and sleep it off, Joe. I swear to you, if you pull something like this again, I'll contact my lawyer and you'll lose the one weekend a month you get with Julie."

Before Joe could respond, the door slammed in his face. The porch light went out, leaving him clothed in darkness.

He remained on the porch for another five minutes before turning and starting back to the car. The rain had tapered to just a light misting, but the saturated ground squelched under his feet and his hair dripped cold droplets down his face.

As he pulled away from the curb, he mused on how much his life had changed since he'd left the house earlier, barely more than an hour ago. Life hadn't been perfect, but whose was? Not perfect, but certainly wonderful. Now he was unemployed, separated or possibly divorced, able to see his daughter only one weekend a month, living with his father, and all signs pointed to his mother being dead. All because of that damn book.

Gripping the steering wheel tighter, Joe pressed the gas pedal and rocketed through the streets. Determination made him fearless as he sped past stop signs, took turns at breakneck speeds, once clipping a mailbox but not stopping to see how much damage was done. He had to get back to his parents' house quickly. He would go down to the basement and sit among the boxes and stare at that wall, *The Pigmalion Pigs* in his hands, until the other him showed up and they could switch places again.

As he sped around a sharp curve, the book slid off the passenger's seat and fell into the floorboard, flipping open to the final page. The happy ending where Patty gets to be herself and everyone accepts her as she is.

The doppelgänger will never show up again.

Of course not. Why would he? The trade had left him ensconced in a life where he had a loving wife and daughter, two living parents, a thriving career. Earlier Joe had thought that life hadn't been perfect, but it certainly seemed so compared to this one.

So he would sit in that basement and stare at the wall and wait for the opportunity to steal his life back. Weeks, months, years—however long it took.

However long.

I JUST WORRY

Gregg and Zeke hid their bikes in the brush and started trekking through the woods.

"Maybe this isn't a good idea," Zeke said.

Gregg glanced over his shoulder. It wasn't fully dark yet, but here in the shadows of the trees it might as well have been midnight. Zeke couldn't make out Gregg's features, only imagine that trademark smirk on his lips. "This is a *great* idea."

"I just worry we'll get caught."

"So what if we do?" Gregg said. "It's not like we're robbing a bank. We're just trying to sneak into the drive-in to watch a scary movie. Trust me, have I ever steered you wrong before?"

Zeke knew the question was rhetorical so he kept his silence, but he could have listed a variety of Gregg's ideas that had landed them in hot water. However, Zeke couldn't say he regretted any of those instances. As Gregg liked to say, if it wasn't for him, Zeke would spend all his time alone in his room with his nose stuck in a comic. Gregg added some adventure to Zeke's life. That was one of the reasons Zeke liked Gregg so much.

Why Gregg liked Zeke was a harder nut to crack.

As full dark descended, the woods actually became brighter in a weird way. Zeke tilted his head up to stare through the canopy of overlapping branches. The moon hung full and bloated in the sky, like a piece of ripe fruit, shedding an insidious glow that snaked down between the branches to frost the surroundings in a silvery light.

"I just worry we'll run into Crazy Joe," Zeke said.

Ahead, his blond hair looking almost white in the moonlight, Gregg shrugged. "Joe's harmless."

Zeke wasn't so sure. Crazy Joe, which is what almost everyone including Zeke's own parents called the man, was a homeless guy who had become a permanent fixture in town, always muttering to himself and gesturing wildly. It was said he lived out in these woods somewhere, making some kind of camp like a hobo or a madman.

Of course, Zeke had never seen anything to suggest Crazy Joe was violent, but he looked scary. Bug eyes that seemed to never blink, long greasy black hair with streaks of gray that made it look as if a nest of skunks had taken up residence on top of his head. He also smelled, an odor so intense it could make you gag from across the street.

No, Zeke didn't like the idea that they might run into Crazy Joe in the woods.

In the dark.

On Halloween.

"This is going to be so cool," Gregg said. "One night only revival showing. I've never seen the original before."

"I have," Zeke said, too softly for his friend to hear.

Zeke had seen the original '70s *Halloween* on television a few years ago, and he'd thought it was a lot tamer than the horror movies they streamed off Shudder. Zeke didn't quite understand why his friend was so excited.

And yet he did. Neither of them had ever been to the drive-in without their parents, and then only to see animated films or superhero movies. It was exciting to be out on their own like this. A duo, a team.

The fact that they were only 13 meant they wouldn't be allowed in the drive-in without adult supervision, and then there was the conspicuous lack of a car. But Gregg said he'd heard there was a breach in the large fence that surrounded the drive-in at the back, big enough for a person to squeeze through.

The main entrance to the drive-in was out on Highway 101, but taking this trek through the woods should bring them up to the back of the fifteen-foot high fence meant to shield the screen from prying eyes that hadn't paid the fifteen-dollars-per-carload ticket price. Even now Zeke could hear the sounds of car engines, voices, music. Excitement thrummed through him like an electrical current, but so did trepidation.

"You know, we won't be able to hear the movie. They pipe the sound in through the car radio."

Gregg threw an arm around Zeke's neck, pulling him close. "You know as well as I do, a lot of people sit outside their cars on lawn chairs and just roll their windows down. If we set up shop near some folks doing like that, we'll be able to hear just fine."

Zeke shrugged his friend's arm off, even though secretly he liked the weight of it on his shoulders. "I just worry we're going to stand out. I don't want to get grounded again."

"*I just worry*. That's how you start half your conversations. You can be a real downer, you know that?"

Zeke stopped walking abruptly. "Then why do you hang out with me?"

Gregg stopped walking as well, first laughing, but then he seemed to realize his friend was being serious. "What?"

"If I'm such a downer and I ruin all your fun, why do you like me?"

"I didn't say you ruined my fun. I'm just ragging on you. That's what we do, rag on each other. I didn't mean to hurt your feelings. For real."

Zeke knew he was being silly. Gregg was right, ragging on each other had become like a sport with them, to see who could come up with the most creative insults. It didn't mean anything, and it never used to bother Zeke.

Yet his feelings toward their relationship had changed over the past year or so, making him more sensitive and awkward around Gregg. Some of the ease between them had been lost, and Zeke knew it was his fault. Sometimes he wondered if Gregg noticed, and if he did, if he suspected the reason for it.

Zeke opened his mouth to offer some lame apology, but a soft rumbling stopped him. At first, he thought it must be just another car at the drive-in, but this was too close. Somewhere out here in the woods with them. And it didn't actually sound like an engine. It sounded more organic than that, like a dog growling.

Like a mad, angry dog.

Gregg obviously heard it too, staring around at all the shadows that hunkered at the base of the trees. Like black shrouds concealing any number of deep, dark secrets. "Maybe we should hurry up, I think the movie started already."

Zeke realized that somewhere in the distance he could hear the distinctive *Halloween* synth score. He could also hear people already shouting at the screen. None of that truly registered, however, not as much as the growling—increasing in pitch and coming closer, closer.

"We should definitely hurry," Gregg said, and the slight tremor in his voice was almost as frightening as the growling itself.

Almost.

They both started walking quickly, not quite a run but verging on a jog. The growling seemed to follow them, matching pace, somewhere off to their left. Eventually, the growing moved up ahead, then in front of them. Gregg and Zeke came to an abrupt halt, and Zeke reached out and grabbed his friend's arm.

"You know," Zeke said, "we could just go back to my house and stream the movie."

For once, Gregg didn't argue or accuse Zeke of trying to chicken out. He just nodded and started backtracking. "Yeah, that sounds fun. Let's do that."

Now they did break into a jog, feet crunching through the dried leaves that covered the ground like a brittle carpet. The growling followed, increasing its speed as they increased theirs. Somewhere up ahead was Hollowback Road and their bikes, and the relatively safe streets of the town they had grown up in. Here in the woods, in the dark, that world seemed distant and hazy, a little unreal like the fading fragments of a dissipating dream. Zeke longed to wake up.

"I don't know if we're going to make it," Gregg said between panting breaths.

Zeke had to agree. The growling was now right at their

backs, and while it may or may not have been only in his imagination, Zeke thought he could feel hot breath on his neck. He had never been so afraid in his life, not even the time in third grade when Boyd Johnson and his friends had cornered him in the boy's room and threatened to beat him up if he didn't dunk his own head in the toilet. And he had been prepared to do it if Principal Fluety hadn't—

Zeke's right foot hit an exposed root, and he found himself toppling over. It happened so fast he didn't even have time to get his hands up to break his fall, landing face-first in the dirt. Luckily, the blanket of leaves was so thick here that it cushioned him somewhat and kept him from breaking his nose. He did strike his chin on the ground, causing him to bite his tongue, the warm gush of blood filling his mouth.

At the same time that he landed, he sensed something flying over his head and he looked up to see a hairy mass sailing past him and landing on the ground about six feet away.

A wolf, Zeke thought. *The wolf that has been stalking us, it just made a leap for my back and if I hadn't fallen, it would be on top of me right now!*

Any relief Zeke felt was short-lived as the wolf turned to face him. The moonlight fell on the animal like a spotlight so that Zeke could make out every frightening detail.

First off, the wolf was huge. A hulking figure as big as a bear, its black fur was streaked with gray. Beneath its bug eyes, a snarling mouth revealed a set of wicked, sharp teeth.

The animal's entire body was tensed, ready to spring back at Zeke who now lay helpless on the ground like one of those stupid, uncoordinated horror movie characters. Zeke tried to will himself to get up, to run, but he remained frozen in place like some unfortunate Greek who looked Medusa in the eyes.

"Get out of here!"

Suddenly Gregg stepped between Zeke and the wolf, holding a large branch he must have picked up from somewhere. Zeke had almost forgotten his friend was there, his world having shrunk to just him and the wolf. But here Gregg was, standing in front of him like a knight in shining armor, brandishing the branch like a sword.

Gregg swung the branch at the wolf, with the force of a baseball player going for a home run. The wolf retreated a few steps but didn't turn tail and flee into the woods. In fact, its growling intensified into an apocalyptic rumble, saliva dripping from its mouth in slimy ropes.

"Get up," Gregg said, and it took Zeke a few seconds to realize his friend was talking to him. "Get ready to run."

Zeke pushed himself onto shaky legs. "Run where?"

"Back toward the drive-in."

"We're going to try to outrun a wolf?"

"You got any better ideas?"

Zeke didn't answer because he didn't. This might be a stupid plan, but it was the *only* plan.

"On the count of three," Gregg said, keeping his voice

low, as if he didn't want the wolf to overhear. "One…two…
THREE!"

He shouted the last word and simultaneously hurled
the branch at the wolf. The animal was struck in the head,
yelped, howled, and staggered back. That was the last thing
Zeke saw before his paralysis broke and he went sprinting into
the woods, moving quicker than he ever had in gym class.
Gregg was by his side, keeping pace. Zeke knew his friend was
faster and could be far up ahead by now, which meant Gregg
was purposefully matching Zeke's speed so as not to leave him
behind.

Up ahead, Zeke could once again hear the soundtrack
to the film, but under his own ragged breathing and pounding
heart, it seemed impossibly distant. Less distant was the sound
of the wolf. It snarled and growled and barked. Being struck
by the branch seemed to have only antagonized and angered
it, so that it was done toying with them.

The animal wanted blood.

And it was gaining on them.

"We're not going to make it," Gregg said, sounding
only slightly winded, whereas Zeke felt as if each breath he
sucked in brought ground glass down his windpipe.

"What do you we do?"

"Higher ground, follow me."

Suddenly Gregg veered to the right and jumped into
the air. He caught the lowest branch of a large oak tree and

swung up onto it, agile as a monkey. He turned and held out a hand for Zeke, who was not nearly so limber and athletic. He caught Gregg's hand, his feet scrambling on the truck to try to kick himself up. In the end, Gregg practically pulled Zeke onto the branch.

As one leg still dangled, the wolf reached the tree and leaped up, sinking his teeth into Zeke's right foot. Actually into Zeke's shoe, the teeth puncturing the thick leather sole. Zeke kicked out and the shoe slid off his foot, sending the wolf toppling back to the ground.

"Keep going," Gregg said, deftly scaling the branches higher into the tree.

Zeke followed. They finally settled on a thick branch, wide enough for them to both sit side by side with their backs against the massive trunk. They just had to be careful not to lean too far to the side. Below them, the wolf clawed at the trunk, sending little shards of bark flying like shrapnel. It made a few leaps up toward the lowest branch.

"It can't get up here, right?" Zeke asked. "I just worry it can climb up here."

"I don't think so. We should be safe."

"But we can't get back down. We can't live up here forever."

"It'll get tired of waiting after a while and move on to find easier prey. I'm sure of it."

Zeke didn't know if Gregg was really sure or not, but

he sounded sure and Zeke allowed his friend's confidence—real or fake—to comfort him.

The wolf continued to clamber at the base of the tree, as if it could scratch its way through the trunk and topple them out of the branches like babies in some cruel lullaby. Zeke tried not to look down, not just because he didn't want to see the wolf, but because he didn't want to remind himself how high they were. Add heights to another thing he was afraid of.

A chill breeze caused Zeke to shiver, and he zipped his jacket all the way to his chin. Gregg scooted closer and put an arm around him. Zeke stiffened, not because he didn't like the closeness but because he liked it a little too much.

"What are you doing?" Zeke asked.

"It's cold, figure we should share some body heat."

It took a moment for Zeke to relax, but then he snuggled up to Gregg's side. Below he could hear the wolf's frustrated snarling, in the distance he could hear the movie at the drive-in, but the predominant sound was Gregg's heartbeat, a drumming rhythm that soothed and calmed him.

"You asked why I liked you," Gregg said, "and it's because you're good for me. You keep me out of trouble."

Zeke couldn't suppress a laugh. "What are you talking about? You're in trouble all the time."

"Well, yeah, but not *serious* trouble. If it wasn't for you, I'd probably be in the hospital or reform school. You are a good balance for me, and I think I'm a good balance for you. We're yin and yang."

Zeke liked the sound of that. He didn't say anything, but he smiled.

Gregg rummaged around in his own jacket pocket and brought out two candy bars. "Dinner?"

As they ate their chocolatey, nougaty dinner, Zeke mused that it was going to be a long night. No way he could sleep in this situation. And yet, listening to the mingled lullaby of the wolf's growling and Jamie Lee Curtis's screams, he eventually fell asleep with his head on Gregg's shoulder.

Zeke awoke to the sensation of falling, but it was only a phantom feeling. He was still securely on the branch. The sun had come up, a milky light brightening the world. Next to him, Gregg was already awake and staring down at the ground.

"Is the wolf gone?" Zeke asked.

Gregg turned to him with wide eyes. In answer, he merely pointed down. Zeke leaned over his friend and took a peak. No sign of the wolf, but at the base of the tree Crazy Joe lay curled in the fetal position on a bed of crunchy leaves. He was stark naked.

Zeke felt his own eyes go as wide as Gregg's. "You don't think he…" Zeke started, but he didn't finish the question.

The two silently began their descent, taking their time and making as little noise as possible. When they finally made the final leap to the ground, they did it on the other side of the tree from Joe.

"Come on," Gregg said in a whisper, "let's get out of here."

But Zeke didn't immediately take off. He walked around the tree, retrieved his shoe, and looked down at the homeless man's prone form. Joe shivered and whimpered in his sleep. Without giving it much forethought, Zeke took off his jacket and laid it across Joe. It didn't cover much area, but it was better than nothing.

When he looked up and saw Gregg staring at him with that smirk, Zeke said, "I just worry he'll catch a cold or something."

"See, another reason I like you," Gregg said, then leaned over and kissed Zeke.

Holding hands, the two boys walked out of the woods. Zeke found himself limping slightly, a pain in the heel of his right foot asserting itself now that the adrenaline of last night had dissipated. It felt like he had been jabbed in the foot with something sharp.

Perhaps when the wolf bit at his shoe, a tooth had actually penetrated the sole after all and nipped Zeke's foot.

Didn't feel deep or anything, so probably nothing serious.

Probably.

But as they made their way to their bikes, Zeke thought, *I just worry...*

Acknowledgments

I have to thank Lee and David-Jack with Slashic for providing a home for this collection. The work they are doing to elevate queer voices in horror is so important.

My husband Craig has always been such a source of support and inspiration, and I thank him for always giving me the push I need to keep at it.

About the Author

Mark Allan Gunnells loves to tell stories. He has since he was a kid, penning one-page tales that were *Twilight Zone* knock-offs. He likes to think he has gotten a little better since then. He loves reader feedback, and above all he loves telling stories. He lives in Greer, SC, with his husband Craig A. Metcalf.